Mine!

He thought she was his. God had other plans.

Shelley Ginn

A W.I.L.D., Inc. Building Mystery, Book One

Contents

Disclaimer

WARNING: This book contains depictions of stalking, psychological manipulation, and trauma. Reader discretion is advised.

Dedication

For my husband,
Who loves like Jesus;
Who lives impetuously like Peter;
Who thinks introspectively like Paul;
and Who lives as humbly as Daniel.

Thank you for your unwavering belief in me and support
-- both emotional and spiritual.

Because Christ Lives! we can love,
   Shelley

Chapter 1

He stands just out of view of his very pretty, petite future wife. Waiting. Longing. Getting very distressed with her choice of clothing. She should know she cannot leave his sight—and ultimately his protection—dressed the way she is. It's not proper. It will not do. What does she think she's going to accomplish wearing that ridiculous maid's outfit? No wife of mine will ever dress or behave in such an undignified manner. Does she have no sense of decency? Why does she think she can go outside where every pervert can see what she's putting on display?

His eyes bulge at the thought of the punishment he will instruct her in. She needs adequate punishment, soon. His head gets even lighter thinking about her crying and plead-

ing for his mercy. Quite possibly a gag will be needed to help her accept her punishment with grace.

Now that I have found the perfect place to train my wife in proper behavior, I need the perfect time.

Not long now. Not long at all.

Punishment is coming.

She. Is. Mine.

Wednesday – Two Weeks Later

Ken Harms checks his watch. Three p.m. Time for his daily inspection. His favorite time of day, he thinks with satisfaction. He loves this beautifully refurbished historic building. He loves his job with W.I.L.D., Incorporated. They have done such an elegant job restoring and maintaining this building and all the unique features, even while turning it into condominiums.

He grabs his clipboard and heads out of his basement office to make his daily rounds. His love of exquisite and excellent craftsmanship allows him to enjoy a job most people would not care to excel at.

"But for me, this is a dream come true. The care required for such a superior building is a task that should never be taken lightly or without care." Ken walks up the stairs

silently thanking God and W.I.L.D., Inc. for the excellent salary that allows him the privilege of caring for this building and its tenants.

"I think I'll start at the top today and work my way down. After all, shaking up my routine will help keep my mind sharp and keep me alert to anything I may have missed at the morning inspection."

He enters the lobby from the basement, glances into The Gym, and offers a small, reluctant wave to Bryan, The Gym's manager.

Bryan smirks to himself and waves back as Ken starts up the two flights of stairs that will take him to the penthouse level—Brock Thorne's penthouse. Ken never enters a tenant's condominium without permission and a work order, but he checks all the common areas and the outside of the property with care.

Checking Brock's small landing and seeing nothing amiss, he heads back down to the second floor. He notices the cracked stained-glass window again and grumbles to himself.

Ken walks down the hallway and notices that the lightbulb Ms. Carley asked him to change is out again.

"Stupid bulbs." Ken eyes the light expectantly, as if it might hold the answer. "Maybe I need to contact an electrician. I'll check my records, but I'm sure I have changed this bulb at least two, if not three times this month alone."

His pride in this building and in this job would allow him to do no less, but he still cannot fathom why it alarms Ms. Carley so. After all, her only neighbors are Bryan Hogan, The Gym manager, and Chase Braddock, a Lewiston Police Detective and best friend to Brock Thorne, a prosecuting attorney, the penthouse owner—and so much more.

"I mean, really, how much safer can she be?" Ken sighs as he realizes that it is probably him that makes her nervous. He has caught her staring at his tattoos. The soul patch and earrings probably don't help her trepidation either.

"Oh well," he observes, "you cannot make all people happy consistently. I've learned that lesson well enough."

Making appropriate notations on his clipboard, he heads down the plush, wide staircase into the main lobby. Time to check in with The Gym and The Laundry for any problems or work orders requiring his attention.

Ken goes into The Gym first. Bryan is not immediately in sight—only about seven women and Emma, Bryan's teenage niece and part-time instructor, are visible doing a spin class. Ken smiles and waves at the friendly teenager and heads back to Bryan's office. Looking over, he sees

Bryan leaning insolently on his office door frame with one of his trademark smirks aimed directly at him.

"Like what you see, Ken?" Bryan teases.

Ken hardens his face in disapproval. "Good grief, Bryan, rob the nepotism cradle much?" Ken shoots back.

"Me?" Bryan barks out a laugh. "You were the one who was flirting; besides, you know she's my niece, bro."

"First of all, I'm not your *bro*, dude. And second, not flirting. Just being nice to one of the sweetest people God ever saw fit to grace His green earth with."

"You've got me there, Ken," Bryan replies, emphasizing his name. "I never really knew my brother or his family, but I have to concede that he raised a pretty great daughter."

They both glance over at Emma and are once again favored with a flash of her breezy and beautiful smile. The next instant, she's right back in her class, pushing those ladies through an uphill climb.

"Ah, sweet youth," Bryan grouses as he turns back to Ken. "Here to check on work orders?"

"Yes," Ken replies slightly tightly, "and before you inform me again, I know you usually email them to me, but as you know, I like to visually check in while on my evening inspection."

"Right—got it. But no, I've got nothing for you today, Ken," Bryan intones with counterfeit sincerity.

Ken looks at him, unsure if he's being mocked. "Okay then," he decides to offer Bryan a bit of grace. "See you tomorrow, then."

Bryan turns to hide yet another smirk on his handsome face as Ken walks out of The Gym and into The Laundry next door.

Jessica is at the front counter filling out a dry-cleaning slip for an elderly customer. She flashes Ken one of her saucy, dimpled smiles while holding one finger up, silently asking Ken to give her just a moment. Ken nods his understanding and looks down to hide his own grin.

Lordy, he chuckles to himself, *Jessica the shameless flirt and Emmy the sweet saint. How in the world did these two ever become best friends?*

With his head down, a black smudge on the tile catches his attention from the corner of his eye. He glares at it with disapproval, as if it put itself on his freshly polished floors. As he's making a notation on his clipboard, he glances around and finds another mark near the entrance.

"Oh, crap," he moans inwardly. "I just polished the mosaic tile in the lobby early this morning. I hope there aren't any scuffs out there too."

He's startled out of his musings by an abrupt "Harrumph" from behind. Ken turns and scoots quickly out of the way for the put-out elderly, maidenly customer. He offers his most gentlemanly smile and a sincere, "Sorry about that, ma'am." She shoots him a dark look and "har-rumphs" at him again as she stalks regally out the door.

As soon as she clears the lobby door and is safely out of earshot, Jessica snarks out a laugh. Ken looks at her and barks out a laugh of his own.

"Maybe I should have gone with 'Miss'," he gurgles.

"Hey, don't worry about it," Jessica grins. "You could have bowed down, kissed the rings on her fingers and her toes, and addressed her as Your Highness and she still would have just 'harrumphed' at you. That's all I ever get from her too."

Ken laughs again and eyes Jessica, wondering just how mischievous she is. Jailbait, for sure, but sassy and flirty to a fault. Instead of chiding her with a well-deserved scolding, he just silently consoles himself that at least she's not his responsibility—therefore her attitude is not really his concern.

Ken grins conspiratorially at her instead. "Okay, Princess, just stopping by to see if you guys have any work orders for me."

Jessica wrinkles her brow and looks around. "Well, I thought Thomas said something about the sink in our bathroom leaking, but I don't see any paperwork on it."

She shoots him a crafty grin. "Are you sure he didn't email it to you?"

Ken offers her an exaggerated, long-suffering sigh before replying, "So, is Thomas here? Or did the mighty laundry manager take yet another afternoon off?"

At that thought, Ken frowns and looks around. "He hasn't left you alone here again, has he?"

"No, *Father Protector,* Thomas is here somewhere. Probably out back on another cigar break," is Jessica's snarky reply.

"He shouldn't leave you here alone. Ever." Ken frowned as a flare of panic briefly crawled up his spine. He stepped behind the counter, pausing to give Jessica a considering look, then headed back to search Thomas out.

Jessica just smiled, then a slight frown marred her brow as she turned to watch Ken walk away with slightly wary confusion. *"Where is Thomas?"* she wonders again. Shrugging off her concern, she gets on with her work, cleaning out the front desk and organizing everything in the lost and found bin.

Sunglasses, gloves, scarves, stuffed animals, underwear? *Seriously?* Sippy cups, keys, etc. And one lone key that looks awfully familiar to her. In fact, it looks a bit like the key to The Laundry. *"I wonder if Thomas has lost his key again?"* she muses as she pockets the key. She packs up the rest of the lost and found items that have been hanging around for months for donation, as another customer walks in the door and her attention is quickly pulled back to her work.

Ken didn't see Thomas anywhere. Too much unfinished laundry for 3:30 in the afternoon, but no Thomas. He looked left and right in the alley out the open side door. Still no Thomas.

"For crying out loud. Where is that jerk?" Ken muttered aloud.

"The jerk is right here, Kenneth."

Ken jumped a foot, letting out a yelp as he spun to find Thomas wiping his hands on a dirty rag.

"Good Lord, man," Ken griped, "stop sneaking up on me, you butt-wipe."
His glance fell to the rag in Thomas' hand and he sighed. "You tried to fix the leak on your own, didn't you?"

Thomas smiled a most insincere smile. "No, not tried—*succeeded*, Kenneth."

Ken sighed impatiently—both at the self-service fix and the formal way Thomas talked down to him—but not wanting to be the first to cave to adulthood, responded, "Move out of my way, ass, and let me check it out."

"Not necessary, Kenneth," Thomas replied with a malevolent grin as he moved aside to let Ken pass.

Ken stepped into the bathroom, turned on the taps, and checked beneath the sink for any leak. Not finding one, he turned off the taps, sighed, and turned back to Thomas. Just looking at his insolent grin infuriated him—a lot.

"Fine. No more leaks. But that's why I'm here. It's *my* job to fix things that go wrong in this building."

Ken eyed the rolling baskets full of dirty laundry. "I do my job so that *you* can do *your* job, idiot."

Thomas quirked an eyebrow. "Really, *idiot*? So far, you've called me a butt-wipe, ass, idiot... and, well, whatever. What is with all the teenage insults?"

A fire burned Ken's face. He stiffened his spine to his full six-foot height, a good inch taller than Thomas, and to the best of his ability, glared haughtily down at the man.

"Oh, shut up, Thomas."

Ken turned and walked stiffly away as Thomas chuckled snidely behind him.

Ken passed by Jessica with a quiet "see you later," not wanting to interrupt her conversation with another customer.

Walking out of The Laundry with a sigh of relief, he again noticed the scuff marks on the floor. This had him with his head down, walking a grid pattern on the mosaic lobby floor, looking for any more marks. He was just noting another on the diagram on his clipboard when he almost bumped into Mrs. Bruns and her son Jonathan coming into the lobby from the main entrance.

"Hello, Ken," Mrs. Bruns offered in her genteel southern accent that made Ken feel loved and cherished.

"Hello, Mrs. Bruns. Jon. How are you both doing today?"

Mrs. Bruns clasped his hand, as was her custom when speaking to anyone she cared about. "We are well today. The sun is shining, the scent of autumn is in the air, and my Jonathan is home with me—alive and well."

Jon smiled a bit sadly. "Well, at least alive."

At his mother's quelling stare, he quickly added, "I'll concede to healing. Not well, not yet. But healing."

Mrs. Bruns turned to clasp her son's large hands. "Dear..." she began, but Jon quietly interrupted her.

"It's okay, Mum. All will be well, in time. How can it not be, with you for my mum? I don't know how, but you always seem to get your way."

Jon's affectionate smile took all the sting she might have felt from being interrupted and contradicted. Before she could begin again, he added, "Hey, I'm going to go work out for a while before dinner."

"Again?" Mrs. Bruns exclaimed. "Heavens, you already worked out for an hour this morning and had physical therapy this afternoon. Are you sure this isn't too much of a good thing?"

"Mum, when is exercise ever bad?" Jon smiled down at her. "Besides, I'm only going to do some mild cardio and probably have a steam."

"Alright, Jonathan," she conceded with a less-than-believing glare. "Dinner, as you recall, is promptly at six p .m." She looked at her watch. "Which gives you exactly two hours and eleven minutes to be at the dinner table. *Presentable.*"

"Yes, Mother," Jon acquiesced with a grin and a buss on her cheek. "I would never dare be late for dinner, let alone improperly attired."

Mrs. Bruns looked exasperated yet fondly after her son as he crossed the lobby to The Gym.

Turning her attention back to Ken, she realized she was again holding onto his hand. She patted it and let him go with a smile.

"Gracious, Ken dear," she apologized. "You finishing up your inspection? And here I have made you late. It's almost four. I do so apologize, dear."

Ken's sincere smile lit her heart. "That's perfectly alright, Mrs. Bruns. You know I don't keep strict hours. Besides, my quarterly report to W.I.L.D. needs to be done by tomorrow, so I won't be leaving for a few hours yet."

"Well, in that case," Mrs. Bruns invited, "I'll expect you here for dinner promptly at six also." She turned abruptly on her heels to enter her condo. Ken understood it was all for show. She knew him well enough to know he would never refuse one of her meals.

He liked to feel loved and mothered again, and he never rebuffed her generous offers—whether food, advice, or liaising with the tenants. He appreciated her more than he ever appreciated his own mother.

Well, to be fair, he never really knew his mother. She left him on a church doorstep when he was two. Not that it matters now. He had the best foster mom.

Mrs. Bruns startled Ken out of his reverie. "Ken dear, I almost forgot—" she had already stepped into her condo and was tilting back out to speak to him, "I do not have any work orders for you today. Don't forget about dinner at six sharp."

With that parting remark, she went back into her condo to begin her preparations for dinner.

Ken turned around with a huge smile on his face as he headed to his office in the basement to get that report done. Before six p.m. Sharp!

As he came out of the shadow of the central grand staircase, yet another one of those accursed scuff marks caught his eye.

"Good grief! What is with the black-soled shoe scuffs all over my floor all of a sudden?"

Irritation lashed at him as he contemplated the likelihood of finishing his inspection and report before dinner. Not good odds.

"Oh well," he sighed, "it won't be the first time I've slept in my office."

He looked back and started documenting the marks again. Back around the other side of the grand staircase, there seemed to be a greater abundance of marks.

He stood in front of the storage door behind the staircase and contemplated the last mark he found. He glanced up and stared at the door in confusion.

What—and who—would have dragged anything into this closet?

The only people with keys are Mrs. Bruns, who is the condominium's on-site manager, and, well, himself.

Since they had already discussed when to bring out the autumn displays, he felt confident it was not her—and he *knew* it wasn't him.

Slowly, and with no small amount of trepidation, he tried the supposed-to-be-locked doorknob.

It was open.

Without knowing why, Ken suddenly felt scared and panicky. He looked down, trying to even out his breathing and forestall an all-out panic attack. He focused on the scuff mark right outside the door, just now noticing how very much like a drag mark it looked.

"Crap."

Make that two parallel marks. One was much fainter but ran parallel to the darker one he'd first noticed. And there, by the corner of the door, was something silvery... shiny. Out of place.

Ken began the process of internally working up the courage necessary to bend down to see what was glinting in the late evening light.

Eerily, from his standing position, it looked like a cross on a chain.

Was it a necklace?

"Oh, boy..."

"Crap. Crap. Crap," he muttered again, more fervently, as he started hyperventilating.

Bending with his hands on his knees, he began chanting, "Breathe in, breathe out. Breathe in through the nose... breathe out through the mouth..."

Whispering to himself as he struggled to compose himself. Ken wasn't certain how much time had passed, but he was finally able to calm himself and forestall a full-blown panic attack.

At least all that therapy is working—that's one good thing.

Self-consciously, he stood and looked around to see if anyone had witnessed his panic. Only The Gym windows were in his direct line of sight from this angle, and he saw no one there.

Still, it was strange.

Foreboding.

Ken looked around again, glanced at what he now thought of as a cross, took a deep breath to compose himself once more, then contemplated the unlocked door again.

As if of its own accord, his hand reached out and grasped the doorknob. It turned in his hand, and his adrenaline leapt up to drowning levels.

As he opened the door—that *should* have been locked, *was* locked this morning at inspection—he held his breath in dreadful expectation.

He stood there, hesitating for a moment, trying to sense anything out of place.

He started breathing easier before remembering them—what he now internally and unconsciously referred to as *the drag marks.*

He raised his left hand to search for the light switch and flipped it up, illuminating the space.

His pent-up breath rushed out of him in a relieved sigh.
Nothing.

Nothing but what *should* be there.

His eyes traversed the area mentally, taking inventory:

The large Christmas tree for the lobby, wreaths, ribbons
hanging on the far left wall. Beneath, boxes filled with
the ornaments and decorations. All the outdoor light-up
decorations follow to the right. All the autumn garlands
and wreaths.

His mind mentally ticked everything off on his checklist
as his eyes traveled along the back of the wall. He had just
come to the patriotic bunting used for all the appropriate
holidays and was about to slide right on by to the giant
Easter bunny that creeped the snot out of him when his
brain finally caught up with his eyes.

Even as his mind computed what his eyes were telling
him, he wasn't sure he'd ever be able to understand it.

"What the ever-loving..."

With alarming speed, his panic returned with unholy
vengeance.

"Oh, my good Lord," he breathlessly uttered. When he
did get his breath back—much to his chagrin—he realized,
in the dim recesses of his mind, that he was clutching the
doorknob and *screaming* like a man with his soul unrav-

eling at his feet, making his whole existence unstable and susceptible to defeat.

There was no way to stop it. No way to even breathe through it until he felt a hand firmly grasp his arm and jerk him around.

Mrs. Bruns lifted her arm to slap him—but that wouldn't be necessary.

Just her and Jon standing there, staring at him in shock, knocked him back into the blistering harsh present.

Mrs. Bruns, openly alarmed and curious, looked at him and began to ask the question Ken already knew was coming.

It was then she noticed how severely he was shaking and panting.

Jon interrupted anything that might have been said. "Mother, he's in shock. We need to get him in the condo and warm him up and probably call the..."

Jon trailed off as he took another look at his mother's ashen, staring expression. He cast a quick look at Ken and noticed the other man pointing to whatever they were both now staring at in horror.

Jon got a horrid feeling in his own gut as other people came running from The Gym and The Laundry.

It was Mrs. Bruns who stopped them all without taking her eyes off the object of her and Ken's attention as she lamented,

"Oh, sweet Jesus. What have they done to you, you poor love?"

"Oh, Ken..." She tried and failed to comfort him as she pulled him into her arms. She turned to Jon, who she realized was now up to speed on the situation. His eyes, usually so kind, were now hard and angry.

His posture and demeanor silently transmitted his Military Police training as he moved her and Ken back from the door.

"Bryan, call the police and paramedics immediately!"

He caught Thomas' eye and silently communicated—like only the military could—to do some crowd control. *Right now.*

Jon turned and, with caution born of police training, shut the door behind him and noted that Thomas was moving to stand guard. The two shared a silent nod and a grave look.

The sight of the ravaged, unconscious girl—stripped, gagged, bound in obscenely tight ropes, coated in blood, and probably, *hopefully*, sweat... and hung by the Fourth of July bunting—was an obscenity the three of them who witnessed it first would never forget...

...nor forgive.

Chapter 2

Screaming startles him. Looking up at the stupid simple-ton's wide eyes, they both glance around, and it dawns on him—this is a scream of pure terror.

"What the...?" he mutters to himself.

I knew better than to leave Carley alone. I knew better! She doesn't have the sense God gave a dog. This must be her fault. There is no way anyone could have ever found her by accident. I had the perfect place to train my wife. Yet if I hadn't come running when this teenage simpleton summoned me, she'd have come looking for me—and that would have been disastrous.

That simpleton is heading out to check out the screaming, and he acts on his self-preservation instincts and follows her. He can think of many ways to punish such a nosey little sim-

pleton. After all, she managed to distract him from his wife long enough for her to temporarily escape her punishment and new life in grateful servitude to him. Now, it's only fair that she takes Carley's punishment in recompense.

With one final look at his new substitute, he takes a deep breath, refocuses, and does what needs to be done now. Plenty of time for Jessica later...

Some days later...

"...any way to know how much longer she will be in this coma, doctor?"

"Do you think she needs more pain medicine?"

"...probably having a dream... wish she would wake..."

"Does Chase have any news... what? More tests? Are you sure they are completely necess—"

"How's our girl doing today?"

Snippets of confusing conversations filter through Carley's consciousness. Softly lit shapes define her current strange, yet comfortable and comforting world. Much like one of the massive blanket-and-pillow nests she likes to build when she needs solace from the world.

Right now, as she passes back into unconsciousness, there is much to be said for not having to think or remember.

***

So many voices have seemed to flow over her for days that she feels particularly tired of listening. One voice seems extremely strident and irritated right now. *Becca. That's Becca,* Carley groggily observes. *Wonder what she could possibly have to be so anxious about. Surely not me. But if not me, then who?*

Carley struggles for clarity. *Don't go there right now, Carley girl,* she hears in a voice that sounds uncannily like her daddy—who has been dead for nine years.

Daddy? Carley pauses to listen, but hears no more from her daddy.

Just as she's settling back into a blessed sleep, lulled by the sweet smell of flowers and the quiet whir and beeps of machinery, Carley's eyes jolt open at the next quietly voiced question.

"Nurse, please, you must have some idea how much longer she will be in the coma."

Brock's deep, resonant voice, tinged with impatience and deep concern, brings Carley fully awake like nothing else on this earth could.

Carley's small gasp goes unnoticed by all—except the nurse.

Lacey Bowman, RN, according to her name tag, clears her throat and grins with just the hint of a smirk as she answers the impatient Brock, "Mr. Thorne, of course I know when she will wake. However, that's for me to know and you to find out."

With sass in her step, she quickly turns and walks out the door, completely ignoring Brock, whose shocked face quickly morphs into anger as he stalks to the door.

"Bloody heck—who does she think she's dealing with?" Brock is livid.

Becca just giggles and sticks out her tongue at him as he scowls.

"What's so funny? You're just as concerned as I am," Brock grouses.

Brock's English-tinged tirade and Becca's mirth are brought up short by a breathy but very clear:

"Brock? Becca? Can you both be quiet? My head is throbbing harder than a Montana winter."

Carley isn't sure what to expect—but it isn't the *profound pain* stretched tightly across Brock's face. And she's definitely not prepared for the *relief* and undeniable *affection* that quickly follow.

Not sure how to respond to what she's seeing on Brock's face, she turns to Becca for some much-needed clarity.

"Umm, where am I? What's going on?"

Becca gazes back at Carley, clearly caught off guard—not by the questions Carley asked aloud, but by the ones she could see *screaming silently* in her eyes. The ones that demand an explanation for why Brock—rumpled and riled up—is standing in what she now realizes is clearly a hospital room.

More precisely: *her* hospital room. A room filled with roses, tulips, sunflowers, plants, balloons, and all manner of cards and pictures drawn by children.

Becca looks back at Carley calmly, takes her hand, and answers the only question she can right now.

"Sweetie, you were assaulted. You've had a couple of surgeries and have more stitches than the Bride of Frankenstein herself..."

Becca is interrupted by Brock's inelegant snort—and the arrival of Nurse Bowman and a tall, distinguished man with silver hair and a neatly trimmed goatee.

"Ms. Lyons, I'm Dr. Holtshouser, and we are sure glad to see you awake. It's very good of you to rejoin us here in the land of the conscious and mildly annoyed."

His half-smile and small side glance at Brock lend humor to this otherwise confusing and slightly insulting exchange.

"I do believe," he continues, "that if you hadn't woken up soon, the nurses would have formed a lynch mob and strung up your handsome Mr. Thorne here by his tongue—and possibly other delicate man parts."

Dr. Holtshouser chuckles at his own wit while Carley nearly chokes on her tongue.

"Wait—what? *My* Mr. Thorne?" Carley shoots Brock a clearly horrified glance that quickly morphs into embarrassment as she looks to Becca for help.

Becca steps even closer to Carley's bed, takes her hand in both of hers, gently stroking it to calm her, and offers a small wink.

"While Brock and I appreciate that you graciously chose us as your duly noted and official ECPs, we have been rather impatiently," she continues—sliding a smirk at Brock, "waiting for you to wake up.

"Seriously, girly, you've been taking your time—and a lot of ours."

Noting Carley's clear look of dismay, she hastens to add,

"Really, Sweetie, Dr. Holtshouser here—and his herd of sycophants—have assured us that your physical condition, while bad, has every indication of a complete recovery. And you survived."

Tears fall from Becca as she continues. "We all knew your assault could have been worse—although not by much—but we've been so worried when you wouldn't wake up for us."

Carley didn't say anything. She was so overwhelmed. Several very important things had just been made very clear.

First, she really hated that she made Becca cry.

Second, the severity of her injuries was obvious—even if she still didn't know what caused them.

Third, pain was becoming uncomfortably evident in every part of her body.

And last—but truly most importantly—she could feel the all-over-body blush rising over the fact that she had *indeed* listed Brock as one of her Emergency Contact People.

She took a swift embarrassed glance at Brock then shot a dark, would be dangerous if not bound to the bed by injuries and what seemed to be 50 lines, tubes, and wires, look at Becca as she muttered, "Geez, why would you bring up my ECP's Becca. Geez Becca."

Silence weighed heavily for a few moments until Brock cleared his throat, looked to Dr. Holtshouser, and—finding no help there—decided absence was the better part of valor in this case.

"I'll be in the hall making some calls. Becca. Carley. Nurse Bowman. Doctor."

He nodded politely as he quietly left the room.

"Yes, well then, Carley," Dr. Holtshouser continued, "let's see what we have going on. You know, besides the waking up bit. That's great and all—but you, young lady, have a journey ahead before you're truly healed. So let's see what we've got going on with you right now."

It did not escape Carley's attention that the look Dr. Holtshouser shot Becca was a clearly confused, silent question. Just what that question was, however, remained unclear—at least until she could corner Becca and get some better-be-very-good answers out of her best friend.

With brisk efficiency, Dr. H—as he insisted on being called—at some point during the last hour of what should qualify as torture under the Geneva Convention, performed every test he found necessary and Carley found exceedingly exhausting.

Becca had escaped to the lounge, and Carley would've felt totally abandoned to Dr. H's obscene joviality if not for Lacey, her day nurse—a woman Carley was considering ousting Becca's best-friend status for. Right now, it would be a tight race that Becca would probably lose... due to Lacey's access to the good drugs.

Carley was succumbing to sleep again, exhausted by just over three hours of being awake after sleeping for... hmm... Carley realized she didn't even know how long she'd been unconscious.

"Ms. Lyons—Carley," Dr. H interrupted her silent musings, "do you have any memories of what happened to bring you to us? Can you remember anything before waking up here?"

Carley began to speak, then paused significantly, as if the question was the hardest one she'd ever been faced with.

"I'm not sure. I know I wasn't driving, because I rarely do. Was I hit by a car? No... that doesn't feel right. Did I take a severe fall? I *am* a bit of a klutz."

With a gentleness and evasion that sent Carley's internal alarms blaring, Dr. H tried again.

"Okay. Why don't we begin with what you *do* remember. What can you tell me about your last clear moments before waking up here?"

In concentration, Carley drew her brows together, trying to remember... well... anything. The only thing she could really focus on was her ever-hovering headache blooming into larger and larger proportions.

"Well," she began, "I guess the last thing I can remember doing is feeding Moose and Squirrel right before putting on my coat to leave for the bookstore. It was my turn to host the Tuesday Children's Story Hour. I guess with all this"—she waved her good arm self-deprecatingly over her body—"maybe I should consider a zombie book instead of *Bad Kitty Takes a Bath*."

She paused, pondering what came next. Out of the corner of her eye she noticed her nurse, Lacey, adding something to her IV line.

"I remember locking my door and going downstairs. I think someone called my name... but I cannot be one hundred percent sure about that..." Carley trailed off in frustrated concentration. "Did I make it to the store? Did I do Story Hour?"

Carley glanced up at Dr. H for clarification, and one look at his face told her what she couldn't remember.

She apparently did *not* make it to Story Hour.

"No, Ms. Lyons, you did not make it out of your building," Dr. H thoughtfully supplied. "Now might be a good time to go over your list of injuries to see if anything sparks a memory. Would that be okay with you, Ms. Lyons?"

"Please, call me Carley, Dr. H. Could I have possibly tumbled down the staircase again? I tend to trip over my own feet."

Carley was trying to hold her panic at bay when, from the door, Brock growled, "*Again?*"

Chase Braddock, one of her neighbors and a Lewiston Police Detective, pushed in behind Brock's still-scowling countenance, followed quickly by Becca.

Brock was still scowling.
"When did you fall the first time? And why in the world am I only hearing about this now?"

Carley shrank back into her bed, unsure how to respond to his obvious anger over a simple tumble down the stairs, when Chase—noticing her trepidation—laid a hand on Brock's arm.

"Not pertinent right now, Brock. Hey Carley, how are you feeling? It's great to see you awake—finally."

"I'm confused, in pain, mortified... and now wondering exactly what 'finally' means," Carley groused her displeasure by pouting prettily.

Dr. H tried to break back into the conversation to continue his examination and explanations, but before he really could, Chase stuffed his foot in his mouth.

"Mortified? Honey, sexual assault is nothing to be mortified about. You did nothing wrong."

"Detective Braddock!" Dr. H and Lacey exclaimed simultaneously, along with Brock's and Becca's "Chase!"

But Carley's shouted "WHAT?" brought everyone's attention right back to her—just in time to see her black out once again.

This time when Carley came to, Brock was sitting on her left, holding her hand, and Becca was on her right doing the same—both sound asleep. A glance at the window told her several hours had passed, based on the reflection of the sun's rays dancing upon the ceiling.

As her gaze slid down the wall, she found Chase sitting on the uncomfortable-looking green chair tucked into the corner, staring at her with remorse and compassion.

"Carley, I'm so sorry," Chase began quietly, in consideration of the two exhausted people napping at her sides. "I had no idea that you hadn't remembered anything about the assault. I'm an idiot who needs to have his lips sewn shut."

Silent tears slid down Carley's face. Chase handed her a handkerchief from his suit pocket as she carefully—and tellingly—disengaged her right hand from Becca's to accept it.

After a swift peek at both Becca and Brock to make sure they were still asleep, she quietly asked the question she didn't really want to have to face.

"So, umm... I was... well, it seems that... that I was... umm... raped then?"

"Oh, honey, no. Not exactly." Chase raked his hand through his hair in frustration before continuing.

"Honey, I'm not in charge of your investigation—I'm your friend and neighbor, and that would be inappropriate. Detective Robyn Hayes of Criminal Investigations is in charge. But I suppose I owe you a few answers now, don't I? Or would you prefer I go get Dr. H back in here? He was pretty pissed at me for screwing up his examination. Not to mention that Nurse Lacey—and by the way, *wow*—can give you more of that feeling-fine juice of hers if you need it."

Carley considered it. "I think I'd rather you just fill me in a bit—not about my injuries, I can feel most of them—and Dr. H would probably get even more pissed at you. But about what happened to get me here? Yeah... I could use a few answers to that. If it would be, you know, okay?"

Carley was dabbing her eyes again with Chase's handkerchief while he considered her request.

"Honey, maybe we should wait for Brock or Becca to wake up... or wake one or both of them up before having this conversation."

"Ah, *no!*" Carley whisper-shouted with an emphatic shake of her head that caused it to start pounding again. With a swift glance at Becca, then Brock, to make sure she hadn't woken them, she hissed at Chase,

"Geez, you cannot just tell a person that they've suffered a sexual assault but were not technically raped and *not* elaborate. Now don't move and quietly tell me what you know before I pull your ears out through your nose."

Chase settled back into his chair and grinned at her.

"You know, honey, it's good to see you in temper again. But threats are not necessary for information. After such a long silence from you, I've got to tell you—what a relief it is to hear you threatening me again."

"Long silence? Just how long is *long*?" Carley questioned, her mouth hanging open like a hyperventilating goldfish.

"Holy crap, honey. Just did it again."

Chase chuckled. "Are you sure you wouldn't prefer someone different—someone better—to talk about this with you? Or, if you wouldn't mind, maybe I could keep out of trouble if you just ask me questions, and I don't really have to think on my own. It might be better for both of us that way."

Carley took a deep breath. "It's okay, Chase. This is not a normal situation. I get that. Why don't you just start, and I'll interrupt if I have questions."

Carley leaned back, closed her eyes, and with a resolute spirit Chase had always admired about her, she opened them again—steady, clear, yet full of torment and determination to face the truth.

And the questions.

Many questions.

"Okay, well... let's do this then."

Chase took a few moments to collect his thoughts, and when he spoke again, his cop demeanor was front and center. And so was his always-present notepad.

Chase's cop voice was strong, steady, and concise, which Carley appreciated as he began:

"At approximately 4:10 p.m. local time on the twentieth of September, Ken Harms, maintenance man for the Westcott Building, located at 337 Adams Boulevard, discovered black scuff marks on the newly polished floor of the lobby that led to the main floor storage closet, which he found unlocked.

"Upon entering and inspecting the storage closet, he discovered you—" Chase cringed in regret for what was to come—"unconscious and apparently severely beaten.

"Mr. Harms screamed, which alerted Mrs. Bruns, the condominium manager; her son Jonathan Bruns; Thomas Mitchell; and Bryan Hogan, among others.

"Bryan Hogan called 911 on his cellphone. Mrs. Bruns' son, Jon—who has military police training—entered the closet to check for your pulse. Upon finding you alive, he told Bryan to request EMTs on the scene also.

"To preserve the scene for officials, Mr. Bruns carefully shut the door after securing Thomas Mitchell, also with military training, to stand guard outside and keep everyone out until police and EMTs arrived.

"Per Mr. Bruns, Mr. Harms, and Mrs. Bruns' statements, you were found naked, bound, gagged, unconscious, and severely beaten.

"Police and emergency personnel arrived within seven minutes of Mr. Hogan and Mrs. Bruns' calls and swiftly took over your scene and stabilization before transferring you to the hospital."

Chase paused.

"It is now the thirtieth of September. You were unconscious for just over ten days."

Chase paused again, giving Carley a moment to absorb all that he'd just ladled on her head and heart. He could see her shock and horror—but also her determination to see this through with as much dignity as she could muster.

Carley inhaled deeply through her mouth and let it out slowly through her nose. She offered Chase a slight wave of her hand to indicate her readiness to continue.

"Dr. Holtshouser was waiting for you in the Emergency Room when you were brought in. He had been called by

Brockton Thorne to take over your primary care—as a favor to the Thorne family, but especially to Brock, who is a good friend of his."

Carley's question was clear in her eyes, and it had Chase backtracking a bit—not wanting to give away all of Brock's secrets, since they weren't his to share. A quick glance at Brock revealed him glaring at Chase, which Chase correctly interpreted as: *Shut up, stupid.*

"Well," Chase hedged, "Brock and Becca were both called by Mrs. Bruns. You had them both listed on your condo application as your E.C.P.s."

At Carley's confused look, Chase explained, "E.C.P. means Emergency Contact Person—or persons. And because you bestowed upon Brock this great honor, and he takes his responsibilities very seriously, he called in Dr. H—and that is that."

Carley's blush and bowed head, along with Brock's clearly questioning gaze leveled at her, clued Chase into the undercurrent of non-communication.

As he continued, Chase murmured more to himself than to Carley, "That one surprised me a bit, honey. I didn't know you and Brock were that close. Or did I miss something?"

Brock snapped his eyes shut just as Carley cut him a look, trying to assess whether he was truly asleep.

"I... well... I don't have any family, and when I first moved here, I only knew Becca," Carley began. "I only used Brock's name because he was one of our first customers at the bookstore, and he was the one who let me know about the open condo in his building. It was a spur-of-the-moment, complete-lack-of-discretion thing on my part—solely because I knew his address. I guess Mrs. Bruns had his phone number, because I didn't have that to list on the form. Anyway..."

Chase cleared his throat and nodded. *Interesting*, he thought. *Alone and unattached. Interesting.*

Out loud he continued, "You'll have to go over all the medical details with Dr. H. I can tell you that you were not raped. Although there were open condoms at the scene, they were unused. The doctors all concur that you were not technically raped. I'm not sure how they can know that, but I'm sure they'll be able to tell you..."

Chase trailed off at the blush slowly creeping up Carley's neck and face—all the way to her hairline.

"Well sure, I mean... yeah," Carley stammered. "I'll be sure to ask him about that. Oh geez."

"Carley," Chase said sternly, "we've covered this. You should *not* be embarrassed over any of this. For crying out loud, you did nothing wrong. You are the victim of an assault—ah crap, I'm sorry, Carley. I'm being an ass again."

He rubbed his face with frustration. "Okay, yes, honey. You were assaulted, but *not* raped. This ass either couldn't get that far or had no time to before you were discovered. However, these are things Detective Hayes will go over with you. In the meantime, I'll have Dr. H get a jump on someone *more professional than me* to talk to you."

Carley's quietly agonized sobs broke Chase. "Ah, crap, honey, please don't cry. I'm just a big ugly cop and have no idea what to do with tears. Apparently all I'm good for today is putting in—and then prying—my feet out of my mouth."

He looked over to Becca in quiet desperation, but she was still sleeping. Then to Brock—who was *still* faking sleep. Chase half-decided to out him, but Carley's half-gasp, half-choked-out bark of laughter stopped him cold.

"Crap, honey! You went from embarrassment, to tears, to laughter. Are you *trying* to kill me here?"

Chase leaned forward, pleading, "Are you okay? Would you like me to wake Brock up? Becca? Maybe grab a nurse? *Crap!*"

"Chase. It's okay. I'm okay—well, maybe not *okay*, but if I can laugh, even a little, then I guess I *will* be at some point." Carley grimaced. "Anyway, you misunderstand. I...

umm... I probably know how they were able to tell I wasn't 'technically' raped."

While a mortified blush crept up her downcast face once again, Brock and Chase exchanged a confused look over her head.

While Chase might be a bit dimmer than Brock on most occasions, light was breaking through the confusion and connections were being made.

Chase grinned over at Brock, who was still trying to hide his befuddlement while faking sleep.

Chase decided to out her—for her own good, *where Brock was concerned*, of course.

"Aw, honey... are you a virgin?"

Carley stared at him in shock, then slowly nodded.

"How did you guess that so fast?" she muttered. "Geez. I feel like such a teenager. The biggest crush of my life is laying here asleep holding my hand, and his best friend is taking potshots at my life. *Crap.*"

Chase shot Brock a clearly challenging look as he quickly grabbed Carley's other hand—the one she'd crushed his handkerchief into—and gently pried her fingers open.

He soothed her hand in his as he added, "You know, that's nothing to be embarrassed about either, honey. In fact, it's... endearing. Especially in this sexual smorgasbord age. I've got to tell you—it's refreshing."

"What it is," Carley said tartly, "is a lack of time, interest, and a date... or five. Not to mention a load of family commitments to deal with since I was thirteen. One thing after another and *bam!* I'm a twenty-six-year-old virgin. Then I became aware of just how precious it is and I decided to save myself for marriage. If God commands it, there is an excellent reason for it."

She smirked at Chase. "You think they'll make a movie about that?"

Chase and Brock both grew still.

Chase jumped in quickly, "Honey, I thought you said you didn't have any family to contact. I mean, with your ECPs... no one ever really checked. But now, if—"

Carley cut him off. "No. No family. Not anymore. My parents were both only children, and I lost all my grandparents within two years of each other when I was young."

Quietly, she continued, "My parents are both dead, as well as my only brother. There's no one."

Fresh tears began to flow down her cheeks. Great, heart-wrecking sobs tore from her throat as her entire life caught up to her in one terrible, spirit-crushing moment.

"There's no one."

Chase looked to Brock for guidance, only to see him gently wrap his arms around Carley. When Brock looked back at Chase, he was startled to see muted grief and anger in his friend's eyes—and the tense set of his jaw.

Startling them all, Becca suddenly muttered, "*Bullcrap.*"

The expletive garnered its intended effect. Carley giggled through her tears, and Becca continued her rant.

"Do you have *any* idea how long I've been sitting here with you and Brock while those two old biddies we hired as part-time help turn our perfect bookstore into a tea shop slash quilting bee gathering place—using our books as coasters?"

She flung her arms wide. "What is that, if not family? *Dedicated* family!"

Carley smiled at her best friend and apologized silently, the way only best friends can do. Becca smiled right back with an all-forgiving grin.

"Truvy was right after all," Carley observed softly. "Laughter through tears *is* my favorite emotion too."

Brock and Chase just looked at each other in confusion—in the way men have been doing for centuries when they don't understand a thing and decide to ignore it.

Becca glanced up at Chase. "How far did you get?"

All seriousness again, Chase replied, "The 911 call and the crime scene description."

Becca grimaced, turned to Carley squarely, and asked point blank:

"Who did this to you? Can you remember who this a-hole is? Anything? Please, sweetie, you *must* remember something."

"No, I don't think so," Carley answered slowly. "I've had a few flashes of color and images... but I'm not sure what I'm seeing. It's just a second or two's worth of jumble. Nothing I can get my head around or understand."

She looked between them all.

"Now that I know some of the details, I'm going to wonder if anything I remember is really a memory of the... of the assault—or just my head supplying one based on our discussion."

"At the same time," she continued, "I *should* know these things. To stay safe. To heal. To just flat out understand what's going on with me—physically and mentally."

Carley shuddered. "Is there anything else I need to know now?"

Brock held her a little closer, his hand resting gently along her shoulder, thumb moving in steady reassurance.

Chase rubbed her hand again. "No, honey. Nothing from me. Dr. H and Detective Hayes will fill you in on the rest—and she'll probably hound your memory, if I know Detective Hayes at all."

He gave her a slight, crooked smile. "Cripes, that woman's a pit bull with a blood-soaked tennis shoe when it comes to her cases. You could not be in better, more capable hands. God help you."

An awkward silence descended while Carley struggled to process everything.

Finally, she snuggled deeper into a surprised but accommodating Brock, and gripped Chase's hand tightly.

"Thank you, Chase. I'll give Detective Hayes all the information I can recall."

She turned her head to Becca and smiled while another round of silent, tearful communication passed between them.

Then, she looked up into Brock's face, trying to ascertain just how long he'd been awake—and how much he'd heard of her and Chase's conversation.

Trying—yet knowing she'd be failing—Carley attempted to obliquely assess his awareness.

"I'm sorry if we woke you, Brock. Is your back sore? I could move over a bit for you..."

Before Brock could answer, Becca broke out into peals of *highly inappropriate laughter*.

"Sorry. Sorry. Well... kinda," she managed between giggles. "Carley, sweetie, you tend to worry about the *strangest* things at the *very strangest* times."

She threw her hands up.

"Seriously, girl. You were sexually assaulted, beaten, tied up, gagged, unconscious for almost ten days while numerous medical tests and surgeries were performed. You were processed by the crime lab and *pictures* were taken—and all you can worry about is whether Brock heard that you're a *virgin*."

Becca snorted. "Carley, I do believe the drugs they've got you strung out on—while they may be fun—have seriously *warped* your perspective."

Carley just stared at Becca in horror while Chase abruptly turned and left—smirking at Brock and trying (but failing) to hide his awkward amusement from Carley on his way out the door.

Becca stared right back, unrepentant and with no small amount of shrewdness in her chocolate brown eyes.

As they glared at one another, Carley became aware of steadily increasing pressure and gentle rubbing on the back of her neck.

Silently, and with intentional precision, she turned her head to find herself staring directly into Brock's gaze.

There was no pity—thankfully.

But there *was* something.

Something that felt like... interest.

Something she had no experience interpreting.

"Clearly," Brock's gentle eyes and words reassured, "that is not the most important thing we need to think about right now.

The fact that you are a virgin—stop blushing, Carley—is absolutely nothing to be ashamed or embarrassed about.

More like *cherished*.

And I, for one, am so very glad that the attacker was not able to take that from you by force.

I will do everything in my power to make sure that never happens."

Quiet tears slid down Carley's face—a face so pale and translucent that any amount of blood flow looked like embarrassment.

Carley felt there was only one option available to her.

She offered Brock a small but genuine smile, snuggled back into his chest, and allowed her eyes to close...

...letting her medications drag her back into unselfconscious sleep.

Chapter 3

How did this happen? The man seethed in white-hot rage. This is unacceptable. He shakes hard enough to rattle any re-maining good out of his soul. How in all that I hold precious did my perfect plan go to Hades so quickly? Never one not to see the silver lining, he reluctantly accepted that at least he saw to her punishment. But he hasn't been able to get their reward for her well-learned lesson. How she must now resent him. He let her be discovered, and now she is under police protection. Of all things!

He knows that it is not her doing; she must be taking a much-needed rest to be ready for him when he comes back for her. That idiot Harms, screaming down the building like the child he is, has been telling everyone who will listen that she was assaulted and almost died. As if. He knew exactly how much punishment his wife could take, and she was fine. She'll be back soon, and he cannot wait to see her face to face again. Right now, his focus has to be on Jessica, that stupid little simpleton. She is in for some punishment of her own. Care is called for. Cops are still crawling all over the building, but right now, his focus is on a certain little simpleton that needs to be seen to. As the rage begins to settle, a plan begins to form. For Carley, Jessica, and maybe even that idiot Harms. His wrath has been stirred into a witch's brew of deceit, pain, and murder. Poison for all...

October 1

The quaint cadence of birdsong brings Carley back from the sweet emptiness of sleep. She takes a quick peek to see if she is alone. Seeing no one, she opens her eyes all the way and begins to take inventory of her room. She has never seen more flowers—real and paper crafted if she's not mistaken—outside of a florist's shop, and the decadence of it all is flattering and brings tears to her eyes. "Becca is right, I do have a family and people who love me. Well, at least my stupid habit of talking to myself aloud is still intact even if my memory is not," Carley sighs.

Resisting the urge to get out of bed on her own when she notices the huge pink boot on her leg: "Well, that had to be

Becca's idea. She knows how much I hate pink..." Carley giggles. "Oh yeah, I'm still getting the good drugs."

Carley raises the head of her bed to take inventory of her injuries. Despite Dr. H's explanations and queries, yesterday was such a jumble of scary revelations that she's not quite sure where all she has injuries. Looking at herself, she wonders if maybe it would be easier to find all the places she was not injured. "Wow. I'm glad right now that I cannot remember anything about this. Thank you, God, for that great mercy."

"So, girl, let's get a sense of what's going on here before everyone descends upon me again." Carley gently probes her sides at her ribs and notices bandages binding her under her charming hospital gown. "Broken ribs—or more likely, bruised." Coasting her hand down to her abdomen, she feels surgical gauze and tape on her right side. Lifting her gown, she stares. "Okay, I knew I had some sort of surgery. Still, that's really disturbing. Okay, right side means appendix, maybe gallbladder, liver, colon. . . I think, and probably something I don't remember or know about."

A headache begins to blossom like poisonous nightshade, making her suspect a concussion—or two, if that's possible—considering the pounding in her brain. She sighed resignedly as she probed her head for any more injuries and unfortunately found her head bandaged and what felt like a lot of swelling and not a little bit of tenderness that extended all the way down the right side of her face. She flinches as she finds the steri-strips there, covering what feels like an unbelievable amount of stitches. As she looks and feels around her body, she finds more steri-strips on both arms, both legs, and if she's not mistaken, on the bottom of her left foot. And to make things even funner, that left foot, in the ugly pink boot, begins to itch. Which only exasperates her further because of course, her left arm is now in a sling. "That's new." It's painful but not in a cast. "So what's up with that? Geez, I bet I'm quite the ugly 'Cinderella' stepsister. As if I didn't have average looks to contend with as it is. Now I'm figuratively Frankenstein's daughter. Swollen, broken, and a virgin. What man could resist that?"

That's when Carley gratefully noticed the handheld trigger for her pain pump lying next to her. "In for a penny, in for a pound," she drolly announced as she pushed that trigger with vengeance... twice. She was ready to have another good cry when something new occurred to her. "Crap, this mess is seriously going to wipe out my savings. I hope this place has a great payment plan. I really wish I'd taken out that health insurance my agent recommended, but nooooo, healthy and happy me could not envision a scenario in which I would need a low-deductible health insurance. Way to go, Carley-girl."

Brock's deep voice resounded from the doorway. "That won't be necessary, sweetheart. W.I.L.D., Incorporated will be taking care of your bills related to this incident for many reasons, not the least of which is that they have great insurance."

Carley shrieked as she whipped her head around to see Brock smiling at her, and she yelped again when pain exploded in her head. Her heart monitor, not wanting to be left out of the fun and games, did some of its own shrieking too as Carley's heart rate exponentially increased. "OUCH!" Carley moaned, clutching her head in her right hand, shooting an evil look at Brock's chagrined face.

Abashed, Brock apologized. "I'm so sorry, Carley. I thought you heard me knock on the door and knew I was standing here. From your reaction, I'm going to go out on a limb and assume that you were not talking to me, but to yourself?"

"Yeah, it's one of my less endearing habits," Carley sighed. "Well, you're here early—what can I do for you, Brock?"

Brock gave her a quizzical look, clearly not understanding Carley. "Carley, I spent the night." Brock nodded to the corner where she just now noticed—through the jungle of flowers—the corner chair was now pulled out into a bed of sorts and had a blanket and pillows piled upon it.

Another jump of her heart monitor accompanied her panicked frenzy of questions. "You spent the night? Here? In my room? Here? Seriously? The whole night? How did I not notice that? Not notice you? Seriously? I mean, those nurses had me up constantly! You were here? Oh, Lordy, I got up and went to the bathroom last night. I mean, I had help from a nurse—well of course you know that, you were here... Ugh!" Carley's manic chattering bombarded a slightly stunned Brock.

Brock slowly started grinning at her complete nervous breakdown. With just a touch of smugness at all that tirade indicated, he took pity on Carley and grasped her hand, soothing it between his own and chose to answer simply, "Yes."

Another jump of that lonely heart monitor connected to his utterly fascinating neighbor increased his smugness and his grin. Carley had no idea what she was in for.

Carley turned her head away to try and gather her dignity more closely around her. "Geez, girl, you act like no man has ever held your hand before. Get a grip! SOOO get a grip."

Brock outright chuckled this time and casually reminded her, "You really should have those conversations with yourself in your head, you know—silently. Especially if you don't want anyone else to hear the conversation."

"Cripes!" she muttered as she unsuccessfully tried to pull her hand from Brock's.

"Oh no you don't, sweetheart," Brock responded tenderly. "I've waited a long time to catch your eye, and while these are less than ideal circumstances to begin a relationship, I'm going to anyway, since I have your captive attention for the foreseeable future."

"I know you've suffered a horrendous trauma," Brock continued, "and you probably scared ten years off my own life, but now that I know you do have feelings for me—and they began long before this business—I am taking advantage. So be prepared, Carley Leigh Lyons, because I intend to take care of you and care for you all the way through this, and hopefully well beyond."

Brock never took his eyes off Carley as he basically outed himself and his heart. "Now, don't panic," Brock responded to the awed confusion he could see rising in her eyes. "This is a deep friendship, for right now, while you're in the hospital. The deepest of friendships. You have a great amount of physical and emotional healing to do, so we go slow. As slow as you need, sweetheart. Right now, I just want to be here for you in whatever way you need and want."

Carley couldn't say a word. She just kept staring slack-jawed at Brock. He was pleased to note that while the awe was still glowing in her eyes, the panic and confusion were abating. If he wasn't way off base, it was being slowly replaced by—well—hope, and maybe a dash of a smug smile as well. He could only hope.

While Carley's head was still spinning and grinning, and Brock was still standing there holding her and staring at her like a love-sick fool, the door opened to a petite, well-dressed woman with a detective shield attached to her jacket lapel.

Detective Robyn Hayes stood at the door and knocked, taking everything in at one glance with her usual crystalline clarity and no-nonsense demeanor.

Carley looked at her warily and politely inquired "I guess you're here for me then. Yes?"

"Good morning Ms. Lyons, I'm Detective Robyn Hayes from the Lewiston Police Department Criminal Investigations Division, and yes, I'd like a bit of your time to ask some questions about your attack now that you're awake. I came yesterday when Dr. Holtshouser informed us that you had regained consciousness. However, you had passed out again after the trauma of discovering you were attacked and Dr. Holtshouser refused to allow you to be woken for questioning. Are you up for it now?" Detective Hayes asked while looking questioningly at Brock.

Carley gave her a small nod and was very glad when Brock slid into the chair next to her and continued to hold her hand. The tiniest thread of panic was once again starting to stitch its way through her head and heart.

"You can call me Robyn or Detective Hayes, whichever makes this more comfortable for you." She smiled at Carley and walked over to the chair on the other side of the bed and opened her notebook. "Mr. Thorne, I didn't expect to see a Prosecuting Attorney here already." She stated with a clear question in her tone and eyes while staring pointedly at his and Carley's linked hands.

"Call me Brock, he offered politely with just a hint of authority, I'm Ms. Lyons good friend and neighbor and I'm here to support her in whatever way she needs."

"Humm." Detective Hayes mumbled and turned her considerable focus back to Carley. "Ms. Lyons, can we start with what you remember from the assault?"

Carley took a deep breath and looked back at Robyn and nodded hesitantly. "Well, it was Tuesday" she begins, "I was due at the store for Chapter Book Story Hour at three pm.

Robyn quietly interrupts, "That would be the Riddled Apple Bookstore on First Street in Historic Old Town that you co-own with one Rebecca Lonely Love?"

"Yes, Carley confirmed. I was dressed as a black cat. The book we were to begin reading was *Bad Kitty Takes a Bath*. The kids in this story hour love that series."

Robyn made a note and continued, "Could you please describe your clothing to me?"

Brock shot her a menacing glare and ground out, "What does that have to do with anything?"

Detective Hayes calmly stared him down and replied, "Mr. Prosecuting Attorney, you know as well as I that *all* details are important."

Turning back to Carley she encouraged, "Would you please describe your clothing in as much detail as you can remember for the record?"

With a swift quizzical glance at Brock, Carley began to think how to describe her cat costume until something struck her as odd. "Don't you have it already in evidence?" she inquired.

"We have several parts of what appears to have been a black cat costume, Robyn reluctantly answered, "but a complete detailed description would be helpful at this time."

"Parts? Okay, parts." Carley repeated. "Well, I had on black leggings with black trouser socks and my black Mary Jane's. I wore a black long-sleeved sweater with a slight ruffed neckline with white fur trim that I sewed on myself. In my hair, I wore a headband with black and white cat ears that I had purchased after Halloween last year. I think that's it. No, I'm sorry I forgot about the tutu."

Robyn coughed and asked, "I'm sorry, a tutu?"

"Oh yes, the girls love them, Carley enthused. Many of the mothers make them for their daughters to match the book theme. It really helps them get more connected with the storyline and enhances cognitive recall of the story."

"Well, that's great," Robyn replied, "but can you describe this tutu please? We have not logged anything labeled a tutu into evidence."

"Sure, Carley agreed with a smile. I use one inch elastic cut to the size of my waist with the ends sewn together. I then purchase the desired color of tulle and ribbon, yards of the stuff. I go the easy way and cut my tulle and ribbon into strips and tie them to the elastic in the middle until you can no longer see the elastic. In the end it is quite a sight.

"I imagine so," Brock responded with a grin.

Carley smiled back at Brock before turning back to Robyn, "The only unique addition I made to this tutu is the black ribbon with white polka-dot tail. I made it by taking a two-inch-wide wired ribbon, cutting it to length, rolling it up lengthwise and sewing it to the elastic. The wire in the ribbon allows me to shape it anyway I need. In this case, a cat tail."

Carley paused for a breath when she noticed Robyn and Brock both staring at her with confused trepidation.

"Are you panic jabbering again?" Brock asked quietly, taking her hand in his to calm her nerves.

"What? No, I am not panic jabbering, she jabbed at Brock with her finger of her other hand. I do not panic jabber, Geez."

Robyn looked back and forth between the two of them with something akin to worry drawing her features taut. "What exactly do you mean by 'panic jabbering' Mr. Thorne?"

"Well, Brock began with a sideways look at Carley, she has been having these tangents when panicked, embarrassed or stressed since she woke up. My belief, and I think Dr. Holthouser agrees with me, is that it is an effect of her pain medication.

Carley looks mutinously at Brock while Robyn merely looks amused. "Okay, she conceded, nothing that will affect her statement to me then."

Robyn turned back to Carley with a neutral expression. "Is that what you were wearing in its entirety? Carley looked at her puzzled. I don't think I understand what you are asking me." Robyn paused, then with her straightforward manner asked, "Were you wearing any jewelry?"

Carley's hand flew up to her throat and she let out a gasp of despair. Tears were falling down her face as she told Robyn, "Yes. I was wearing a silver cross necklace that had belonged to my dad. I haven't taken it off since he died." Brock gathered Carley into his arms soothing his hand up and down her back, giving what comfort he could. "I'm so sorry Carley." he lamented with her, "we'll do our best to find it."

Robyn looked through her paperwork and drew out a single photo and turned it around to show Carley. "Is this your necklace?" Carley grabbed the photo out of the detective's hand exclaiming "Yes!" with elation and joy. "Oh thank goodness, when can I have it back?" Robyn glanced at Brock and then told Carley "It's going to be some time before you get it back. It's now evidence."

Carley buried her face in Brock's chest and sobbed anew for a few moments before gathering herself. Turning back to Robyn, she offered an apology. "I'm sorry. I know it's not your fault or your rules. I'm just feeling overwhelmed.

Please forgive me. Do you have any more questions for me?"

Robyn considered Carley for a moment and decided to take her at her word and finish her questioning. "I am given to understand that you walk eight blocks to the store every day. That's a long way to go in only a cat costume, isn't it?"

"Oh, well, yeah, Carley clarified. I was wearing my calf length coat also. I'm sorry, I sort of thought that was a given. I mean, do you mean to tell me that you think so little of my intelligence that you believe I would walk those eight blocks in the cold with only that silly cat costume for warmth and without my coat? Seriously? Geez."

Robyn faintly smirked. "Well, you would be surprised what some people will do for attention."

Brock growled, Carley stared blankly, and then anger set in. "Well, not me! I was on my way to read a book to children, not pole dance on the corner stop sign!"

Robyn back peddled slightly, putting her hand out to Carly in a placating gesture. "I'm so very sorry Ms. Lyons, that was in no way a shot at you. I was thinking of someone else."

Carley nodded slowly as a grim look turned into a slightly hysterical giggle. "I cannot believe I just said that." She shot Brock with a mild apologizing look. "Okay, maybe

I do panic jabber a bit, but I cannot believe I said that. Seriously, who would want to see me pole dance on the corner stop sign? I mean seriously?" she burbled as another panic jabbered drug induced giggle escaped captivity.

Robyn smiled at her hesitantly. "There is nothing wrong with standing up for yourself. In fact, from what all your doctors tell me, you put up a heck of a fight with your attacker. I'm just a little surprised, glad, but surprised that you have any sense of humor, drug induced or not, at this time."

"Well, I guess if I remembered anything about the attack, I probably would be crying like a baby. I guess amnesia has its good points." Carley acquiesced.

Robyn grimaced. "You really don't remember anything, do you? Nothing at all? The tiniest detail could be very important."

Carley breathed out a whisper of a sigh. "Well, I remember getting ready. I fed Moose and Squirrel and chatted with them a bit. Put on my coat", Carley closed her eyes in concentration as she continued, "made sure my coat was buttoned and securely tied closed. I grabbed my satchel from the entryway closet. Left my condo, locked the door and put my keys back in the satchel. I turned and headed down the stairs, then...nothing. Nothing until I woke up yesterday and all the chaos that ensued from there."

"Wait, wait, wait! It's a tiny thing but you want everything, right?" Carley cried out excitedly.

"Most definitely." Robyn encouraged.

"Well, as I was going down the stairs, I noticed these little white pieces of paper in a trail all the way down the stairs. I had thought to pick them up, but was running late and I knew that Ken, ah, Mr. Harms, would take care of them during his afternoon inspection." Carley paused, thinking for a moment that seemed rife with importance. Brock and Robyn remained quiet as they observed Carley's faraway look and thoughtful expression.

At length, Carley finely mumbled, "I think something, or someone caught my attention during my internal debate about picking up the white pieces of paper on the stairs, but I just cannot think of what or who it was...I'm pretty sure it wasn't anything scary or unusual, but something."

Robyn and Brock continued to sit quietly waiting to see if anything else came back to Carley, but eventually she looked up and inquired of Robyn, "Is any of that helpful?"

Robyn encouraged her with a firm "Yes, I'll be able to build a better timeline with that information. Especially when I corroborate with Mr. Harms and his inspection reports on timing." She quirked an eyebrow at Carley. "Umm, but Moose and Squirrel? Who or what are they?"

Carley squirmed. "Uh yea, Crap, well, they are sugar gliders, a pair of females. Some people recognize them better when called flying squirrels." Carley bowed her head and blushed. Looking hesitantly at Robyn she inquired, "Can we keep them out of any official record, please? I'm not supposed to have any pets in my building, but, well, sometimes I get lonely, especially at night when I do most of my creative work at home. You know, because they are nocturnal and all and give me something cuddly and fun to play with when I get blocked and need a distraction."

"Well, okay then. Moose and Squirrel, the sugar gliders. I'm gonna have to Google that one." Robyn smiled. "I'll try to keep them out of my final report, but if it somehow pertains to the attack, and at this point I don't see that as likely, I'll keep it quiet." She promised.

"By the way, what do you feed those things? Bugs, grubs and berries?" Robyn smiled craftily at Carley.

"Oh no, oh no, oh Good Lord no. They haven't been fed for days. Oh crap. What am I going to do? I guess I'll have to bite the bullet and call Mrs. Bruns to feed them."

Carley's mounting panic was obvious to both Brock and Robyn until Brock gently pressed his free hand over her mouth and at the same time put his finger under her chin and turned her head around to face him. "Sweetheart, it's okay. I've been feeding and caring for them. If I'm not there

I've hired a professional pet sitter to come and see to their needs every day."

Carley just gaped open mouthed at Brock until she realized that he had to have been in her condo to take care of her pets. "What?" she cried. "When, I mean how...shoot...who are you going to tell? Oh Fudge, just tell me how you got into my condo and are they doing okay? Do they miss me? How did you know what to feed them? Did..."

Brock replaced his hand over her mouth, "Seriously Carley, these jabbering micro-bursts cannot be good for your blood pressure. He nodded to her sky-rocketing heart monitor. I'll explain everything about it to you when you are done with Detective Hayes, okay?"

Carley calmed down with a sheepish smile and an equally sheepish "okay" to Brock as she turned her attention back to Robyn. "I'm sorry, what else do you need to ask me?"

"Well just for full disclosure and clarity for my investigation, Robyn asked Carley as she darkly eyed Brock with a not so subtle command in her eyes for him to remain silent, were you wearing any under garments, specifically bra or panties, under your costume?"

"Of course, black for both." Was Carley's instant reply. "Why?" she inquired with more than one question emanating from her eyes.

Still giving Brock her patent stay quiet glare, she answered Carley as carefully as she could. "Well, they were not found at the scene. And according to your description of your costume, she paused to check her notes, the tutu and tail are also missing. Everything else has been cut with a knife, we think. Quite possibly the same knife used, well, on your body. The Crime Scene Unit, or CSU, is still checking that out as well as still processing the evidence that was collected."

"Speaking of which, would you mind if one of the investigators returned to photograph your injuries now that you are conscious. It would be good to document the full extent of your injuries and subsequent treatments required. We will also have to have you fill out a medical release form so that we can get all your records released into evidence. And a list of all medical interventions necessary for your full recovery."

Robyn paused, then continued, "You do realize that photos have already been taken here in the emergency room when you were first brought in as well as all the crime scene photos. You, of course, are not in any of those, but it does graphically paint a picture of what you went through. I thought it would be a good idea to document your recovery in photos for the eventual trial.

Carley thought for a moment before commenting, "I really don't understand who could hate me so much to cause me this much damage and pain. I just don't see this as anyone I could know."

Robyn glanced at Brock, softening her voice she responded to Carley, "We cannot rule out any of your friends and acquaintances. It is more than likely that it will be someone you know, if only very casually. While we are on the subject, has anything, no matter how small or trivial to your thinking, happened in the last six months or so?"

Carley sat pensively for a while. In the meantime, Brock had a few questions of his own for Detective Hayes. "Any leads, Detective? Brock began.

Detective Hayes eyed him warily and responded with "You know the rules Mr. Prosecuting Attorney. I cannot speak with you about this case, not now and not unless you are assigned this case, which I seriously doubt. Considering your personal involvement here."

Anyway, we are still conducting interviews and considering Ms. Lyons was unconscious and now her amnesia, well, it's not looking to be the quick resolution we all want."

"Fair enough." Brock complied. "Well, can you tell me then if you have cleared anyone? I intend to take her to my home for recuperation when she is released, and I don't want to just waltz her back into the lion's den. Is it safe for her to go back to our building?"

"Again, Brock, I don't know how to answer that. You know these answers yourself already. We are, of course, interviewing, confirming alibi's, and checking backgrounds on every tenant and employee in the Westcott Building. However, as you are already aware, the Corporation and the 'owner' of the building have already done this," Detective Hayes stated plainly, looking into Brock's eyes with her patently all-knowing glare. "They have been unbelievably helpful for a major corporation...Thanks, by the way."

Brock's glare had zero effect on Robyn, who thought it was silly to hide such a detail as being the owner of the Westcott Building and many more in the area. Robyn subtly nodded and promised Brock, "I will keep your secret, as much as I'm able to, much like I'll keep Moose and Squirrel a secret from the landlord, Mrs. Bruns, for Carley."

Robyn's smirk sort of pissed Brock off, but not too badly since he knew he could count on her discretion to keep his secret. "Thanks," he said gruffly.

They were interrupted by Carley who raised her voice slightly to get their attention. "Well, she inquired of Robyn, do you really mean *anything*? Because there is a difference between everyday rudeness and intentional malice. So, I ask again, do you need to know everything no matter how trivial?"

Robyn grasped Carley's hand and held it gently. "Carley, sometimes one person's everyday rudeness is another person's malice toward his or her fellow man. I, and all those investigators I have running around, are being very diligent and nosy on your behalf, we need to be the judge of what is rudeness and what could be hiding malice. Okay?"

Carley squeezed Robyn's hand, nodded once and began, "Well, about a month ago at the bookstore, Becca was taking her turn at story hour. It was girl's night, so it was a Thursday. Well, we had one mom that just wanted to drop her little girl off and come back in an hour to pick her up. Becca, trying not to interrupt story hour or embarrass the woman's daughter, sent her over to talk to me. I patiently explained and showed her the sign we have hanging saying that she cannot leave any child unattended. We would have to call the police if she did leave her child."

"I cannot express to you just how well that did not go over." Carley continued. "This woman pitched a hissy fit to rival one of Becca's. She complained loudly and ignorantly for the entire hour. Let me tell you, she made a right bloody 'Karen' of herself and embarrassed her child enough that social services should have been called for that alone. Gracious, just thinking about it again makes me sad for that precious little girl all over again."

"Do you remember exactly which Thursday this was?" Robyn asked as she let go of Carley's hand to make some notes.

"No, Carley sighed. But I do know the little girl has been back at least a couple more Thursday's, with a sitter," Carley added with a grin. "I'm sure she bought books the times she has been in, and we always have registration forms from our story hour participants so Becca should be able to help you get the mother's name and address. Is this really the kind of thing you're looking for?"

"Right now, we are looking for anything and everything out of the ordinary or unusual. Have you thought of anything else Carley?" Robyn asked.

"Yeah, kind of." Carley elaborated and idly retook Robyn's hand into hers, "The only other incident I can think of is from one day the week before the, umm, incident. Umm, Wednesday, I think. Days and dates are kind of hard to wrap my brain around again yet. Anyway, someone bumped into me really hard at the crosswalk at Second Street and Adams. I almost lost my balance right in front of an SUV going well over the speed limit. When I turned around to see who bumped me and maybe give them a piece of my mind, I found five other people there with me all not seeming to pay me any attention."

Carley paused, trying to remember the details. "One young man had his headphones in, and his eyes closed. There was a man reading his paper, a woman on her cell phone, and another woman reading on her Kindle with her young son in tow. With all those non-likely people to choose from, I brushed it off as an accident, but now, well, I guess I'll let you decide that for me.

Brock growled quietly and pried Carley's hand from Robyn's. Robyn in turn looked at Carley incredulously and made notes in her notebook.

"What?" Carley's defenses were up as she tried to yank her hand from Brock's. "You two may automatically assume everyone who bumps into you is out to kill or maim you, but I prefer my rose-colored glasses stapled firmly to my nose and give everyone the benefit of the doubt. I stand by my father's motto. 'Where there's a question of intention, it is better to assume an attitude of redemption'."

"Nice." Robyn stood and shook Carley's hand with sincerity. "I firmly hope that your father is right, but I don't have the luxury of assuming so. I'll check into these two incidents, and you be sure to call me if you remember anything else."

Robyn handed Carley one of her cards. "By the way, I don't think it would be a good idea to go back to the West-cott Building alone." Detective Hayes looked significantly at Brock as she walked out the door.

As a purely stubborn look of consternation crossed Carley's face, Brock quickly interrupted her incoming tirade before it could even begin. "Hey, Carley, not to mention all your medical needs that will need to be met, there's the huge issue of your safety. Detective Hayes is not wrong. You were attacked in the building where you live. She is working diligently to clear everyone who lives and/or works in the building, but that's only part of the issue. You must remember that we live in an open building with two businesses', The Laundry and The Gym, that depend upon outside customers to survive."

Carley's consternation faded and sadness invaded. "I don't have anywhere else to go. Well, I suppose I could stay with Becca, but I have the girls to look after also."

Brock issued another growl. "Carley, you are going to stay with me...without any resistance. I know it's the same building, but I have additional security on my floor and cameras in and around my condo, including the rooftop garden. Moose and Squirrel can stay too. No arguments allowed." Brock showed his resolve as he too walked out the door, forestalling any resistance from Carley.

Now it was Carley's turn to growl, only there was no left to hear her frustration.

Chapter 4

October 6

He eyes that simpleton Jessica with such malice it is a wonder she doesn't just spontaneously combust. He is a patient man—usually—but this is getting ridiculous. It's been over three weeks and still no sign of his Carley.

He got to The Gym two hours ago, working out, waiting, and watching without arousing suspicion. No one is paying attention to him, much to his relief. Bryan isn't here—only Emmy—and she's no threat. She hasn't even noticed him as he quickly and quietly leaves by the back entrance through Bryan's office.

He stands silently in the darkening gloom of early evening in the alley. Fortune is finally smiling on him, and he takes it as a sign. Jessica has just come out of the back door of The

Laundry to leave for the day. As she walks down the alley to her car in the back lot, she doesn't even notice him—partly due to the unobservance of youth, but more realistically due to the earbuds in her ears, with music screaming its way through her simple brain. She has no chance of escaping him now that she didn't see him waiting in the shadows.

With anticipation, he pulls down the mask over his face as he steps out of the shadows to follow.

Carley woke up to low voices elsewhere in the condo. She felt a surge of panicked adrenaline before she remembered she was in Brock's condo—and not only that, she was in his bed.

She rolled over gingerly and snuggled one of his pillows, murmuring to herself, "I am so in Brock's bed. Enjoying his sheets and his scent, and what a divine scent. Lord, take me now while I am this blissed out."

"I'd rather He didn't just yet. I'm nowhere close to having you this close by and not being married to you in this lifetime yet," Brock asserted from the door. "Sweetheart?"

Carley felt a mortifying blush flood her whole body as she desperately clutched the pillow to her. "I don't suppose this is a dream. Please?"

With a definite grin in his voice, Brock assured her she was not dreaming. "Sweetheart, I absolutely adore that particular idiosyncrasy you cannot seem to control. It gives me more than a little hope that you are possibly more than fond of me, too."

Carley carefully rolled onto her back and calmly stuck her tongue out at Brock. "Stop being so smug. It makes you way too cute while I'm lying here with bedhead, breath bad enough to kill gremlins, in desperate need of pain medication, hot soothing water, and soap. In that exact order."

"Well then, I guess it's a good thing I came by when I did." Becca peeked around Brock and grinned. "And while we are making your hair, breath, and body more presentable to human company, you can fill me in on all these clandestine conversations you've been having with yourself and without me—yet still within Brock's hearing. You know, as your duly recognized best friend, that is patently unfair, and I plan to file a grievance with the union. Come on, let's go and dish while we wash you, girl."

"Geez, you startled me, Becca. And that was lame... wish I'd thought of it first. I could use such a line in my new book. That aside, I really do need some help getting up and getting clean. I feel like such a weakling. I can do almost nothing for myself yet. I've only been one day out of the hospital, and I think I am truly spoiled by all the great care I received there." Carley tried to affect a pout while trying to suppress a grin. "Thanks, Becks."

Brock crossed the room and helped Carley up from the bed. "The bathroom is through this pocket door and to the right," he said, pointing behind himself as he steadied Carley with his other hand. "You'll find towels and all appropriate pampering supplies in the linen closet. Carley's clothes are in the back of my closet—in the top three drawers and hanging on the clothing rod to the right."

"Umm. Wow. Okay. Thanks, Brock," Carley mumbled, embarrassed once again. "Wait. What! Hey, how did that happen? Geez."

Brock smiled. "Well, it was magic, really. I got your spare keys from Mrs. Bruns last week, remember? To take care of Moose and Squirrel. Then when Dr. H said you would be coming home, I went back to get your clothes and voilà—here they are."

Roses bloomed on Carley's cheeks again. "You went through my clothes? My dresser? My closet? Why—why would you do that? Oh, geez."

Brock feigned incredulity. "I'm sorry, I just assumed that you would prefer not to stroll home naked from the hospital, let alone around my condo."

"However," Brock smiled, "if that is what you prefer, go for it. Maybe we can all join in. You know—declare my condo a clothing-optional zone."

Becca grinned and smirked at Carley's face. "I'd be glad to go with that. I can start right now, as a matter of fact." She reached for the hem of her sweater.

"What?" Becca said, responding to Carley's mutinous glare.

"Oh, I'm so sorry," Carley snarked. "Did I roll my eyes too quietly for you to hear? Let me help with that." Carley rolled her eyes with extreme exaggeration and emphatically announced, "There will be no optional clothing-free zone here. Ever."

Carley paused, considering her statement. "Well, you know, except for the bathroom, getting changed, or, you know, if you live here and prefer that—well then, that's your prerogative."

With her blush back in full force and Brock and Becca grinning like fools at her, she told herself—not quietly enough—"Geez, shut up, Carley. Just. Shut. Up. Darn..."

Becca strolled over to the bed and rolled her own eyes with great exaggeration. "Yes, please do shut up. Now I understand what Brock is talking about—personal internal conversations remaining such. I've never known you to ramble on so embarrassingly before. You must really, really like Brock. Come on then, let's get you all prettied up so he knows how much you care."

"I hate how much you are enjoying this, Becca," Carley grumbled. "You are way too happy about this to live. Holy bologna."

"I know I am enjoying the heck out of it," Brock supplied with a decidedly loud guffaw.

"Rolling eyes out loud again here, people—at a shout, really," Carley cut in on their laughter. "Becca, please just help me into the bathroom. I'm still sore all over." Carley whined, hoping to end this embarrassing conversation with a little well-timed self-pity.

"I'll leave you ladies alone then," Brock said as he walked over to the bedroom door and slid it closed on his own smug grin.

Becca grinned wickedly at Carley. "I love how something so terrible can lead to something so wonderful. I'm sure he loves you, Cars."

"What?!" Carley shouted. She caught herself and, more quietly, restated, "What? How can you know something like that?"

Becca looked at her in wonder. "Well, let's count it out, shall we? One, you are living—even temporarily—in his penthouse condo. Two, he came to the hospital as soon as he was called. As a matter of fact, I heard he was in court when he got the message and immediately asked for an indefinite recess, which the judge granted based on the level of Brock's distress and the circumstances surrounding his request."

Becca smiled smugly at Carley's shocked and bewildered face as she continued.

"Three, he was at the hospital before me and had his own personal physician there immediately. Four, he is making sure W.I.L.D., Inc. is picking up the bill for all this. Five, he never left the hospital while you were in the coma. Heck, he only left your side for the most basic of needs and for the shortest amount of time humanly possible. Six, even when you woke up, he was there every day. And lastly, he pretty much said so not ten minutes ago—are you deaf, girl?"

Becca had gotten a shell-shocked Carley into the bathroom and undressed during her tirade, when practical concerns brought her up short. "Hey, what about all your staples, stitches, Band-Aids, and various medical paraphernalia that is now tormenting your body?"

Carley just gaped at her, unsure how to respond. To any of it.

"Hey girl, snap out of it. What do we do with all your beautiful accessories?" After all, Becca's patience did have its limits, and woe to anyone—be they broken or whole—who breached the wall of impatience that inhabited Becca.

"Oh, well, all the stitches and staples were removed a couple of days before I left the hospital. Don't you remember? The boot on my leg can stay off for the shower. The doctor put in an internal fixation and it's just for support when I walk around a lot until it fully heals. And I only have to wear the sling when my shoulder is hurting—and it's not hurting now, so no worries there. We can take the bandages off now also. The incisions should be well scabbed over, and the Band-Aids make me itch worse than any of the incisions or cuts. I'm still sore, but I'm hoping that a nice warm shower will help with that. So, I guess that makes me ready to get wet."

There was a brisk knock on the bathroom door as Brock slid it open a crack. "Hey, the pharmacy just sent over her medications. I thought she might need her pain medication, and she's due for her anti-inflammatory and antibiotics."

As Becca and Brock conversed through the crack of the door, Carley took a few moments to look around. It was a truly magnificent bathroom. "Hey," she interrupted, "do you have a chair we can use in the shower? I probably won't be able to stand for long on my feet."

Becca rolled her eyes at Brock. "Thanks. Just leave it all there and I'll get it in a minute." She winked at Brock. "You sure you haven't drugged her already?"

"I'm sure," Brock replied dryly. "Her last dose of pain meds was—" he consulted his watch— "seven hours ago. She's due for her next dose. Overdue, in fact. I'll leave those out here too."

He spoke over his shoulder, making sure to protect Carley's privacy. "Have a great shower, Carley."

"Did he just see me naked? Scabbed, bruised, and ugly naked?" Carley moaned.

"No." Brock reassured her. "No, but I'm sure you are so beautiful, Sweetheart. Simply beautiful," he answered for himself through the door, while Carley groaned in embarrassment. Again.

Becca smiled wickedly and sniggered at Carley's dismayed countenance. "Hey, if he can see any beauty in all of your scars, bruising, and possible mental health consequences you may have through all that—" indicating Carley's marred body as a whole with a wave of her hand—"then you are the luckiest woman in history." Becca's pout was a little sad and a little jealous.

Carley's sympathy was back in force. "Jon still hasn't noticed you yet?"

"Oh, he's noticed me, Cars. He just doesn't like what he sees in me." Becca pouted.

"Nonsense. How can you possibly know that? I don't believe for one second that he ever told you such a thing." Carley turned the water on in the shower as she continued, "You know perfectly well he has noticed you and likes what he sees. You're hard to miss, Sweetie. You're beautiful—with all that glorious black and purple hair and beautiful tattoos. There is no way he hasn't noticed those."

Becca opened the door to retrieve the bath chair and Carley's medication, both delivered by the pharmacy. "I'm pretty sure those are the exact things that have turned him off me. He keeps giving me these strange, condescending looks."

Becca placed the chair into the shower and shook out a pain pill, anti-inflammatory, and antibiotic for Carley to take. As Carley walked into the enormous shower, swallowing the pills with the water Becca handed her, she slid the chair directly into the stream of warm water and commented back to Becca sarcastically, "He looks at you funny? Really? That's your basis for thinking he doesn't like you?"

Becca pulled a face while Carley luxuriated under the water, completely ignoring her, and continued, "You think my head's in the sand where Brock is concerned? Sweetie, you are drowning in quicksand if you believe for one minute that those are 'condescending' looks and not 'I don't know how to talk to this woman and I really, really want to' looks."

"He so wants in your life, but as long as you're still letting Bryan Hogan in, you're not going to get anywhere with Jon. He won't poach on what he perceives as another man's territory."

Carley turned slightly then and held her hand out for the soapy washcloth Becca was holding and found her gaping at her. "Territory?!" Becca screeched. "He thinks of me as territory? That conceited idiot!"

"Geez, Becca," Carley moaned, "stop putting my words in his mouth. It's only that he's an ex-Marine, and according to his mom, he's had honor pounded into him from birth—and the Corps ingrained it even deeper. He's an honorable man. Not one thing wrong with that," Carley asserted. "He won't even approach you as long as you're seeing Bryan."

Becca yanked the removable showerhead from the wall and tipped Carley's head back none too gently.

"Hey! Ouch!" Carley yelped at her.

"Crap! I'm sorry, Carley. I just forgot for a second how much that would hurt you. Are you okay?" Becca apologized emphatically.

"Of course. It's just my head is still sensitive—not to mention that if you pull too hard, you're likely to scalp me, Becks," Carley soothed. "I know you didn't mean to hurt me. Just tell me what you need me to do. Even if what you need is for me to shut up."

Becca was silent for a few minutes as she concentrated on washing and conditioning Carley's hair. "No, I need to hear it. Who ever thought I'd be chasing an honorable man? I mean, I think I already knew that I must stop playing games with Bryan. I'm pretty sure I'm scared to grow up and have a real relationship." Becca sighed heavily. "It's not like I want to have kids with either one, and since love is such a foolish notion, I cannot fathom why I want Jon to see me as something other than a witch with purple hair and weird tats." Becca sighed again as she rinsed Carley's hair.

Carley was prudently silent while Becca finished with her hair. When Becca nudged her gently on the back, Carley handed her back the washcloth. While Becca rinsed and re-lathered it, Carley asserted in a tone of authority, "Alright, first off, honorable in no way means condescending. It does not mean judgmental, nor does it mean wanting to have kids or that he's in love with you. Only he can answer that. But since you haven't allowed him to get to know you, I'm guessing that no, he does not love you... yet."

Carley just smiled to herself as Becca's only response was to scrub her back a bit more roughly than strictly necessary. Carley ignored it as she continued, "What it does mean is—first, he is interested in getting to know you better. He probably wouldn't mind a kiss or two at this point. But most importantly, he will not approach you while you are 'seeing'"—Carley brought out the oft-criticized air quotes as she continued—"anyone else. It's not a 'Bryan' thing; it's a 'you're not available' thing." Carley noted, with air quotes flying all over the room.

"O. M. G.," Becca groaned. "Enough already with the air quotes—I get it. And now that I've had someone explain it to me, it's kind of sweet, you know. I'll give it some thought, okay?"

"Okay," Carley agreed. "And if you're done scrubbing the skin off my back and butt, I'm getting sleepy and slightly dizzy. I think it's time to get done here and out of the shower."

As Carley reached out and turned off the water, Becca walked out of the shower to grab a couple of towels. She had Carley dried, re-bandaged where needed, teeth brushed, legs and everything else that needed shaving, shaved, and into pajamas and sitting on the bed brushing her long strawberry blonde hair in thirty minutes flat.

"Thank you so much, Becks. I feel so much better," Carley mumbled drowsily, falling asleep sitting up as much from the meds as from Becca's expert hair-brushing skills. "I love to feel this clean again," Carley continued to mumble. "Those hospital showers were just not the same. Thanks again, Becca."

"Anytime, Sweetie—just give me a call when you need me. Although I'm sure Brock can help you with basic cleanup, if necessary."

"I can see the blush climbing up the back of your neck, but I don't think this is the time for embarrassment, Cars." Becca continued brushing her hair gently while she spoke in a soft voice. "I know you've been in love with the man for years. Almost as long as you've known him, I think. I also think he's very much in love with you too."

Carley's head jerked up, all sleepiness gone, but Becca overrode her objections. "Just because I don't believe in the institution of love doesn't mean that you two don't."

"Carley, Sweetie, please don't waste any more time—just tell him how you feel already. As we've all recently discovered, life here on planet Earth is not eternal nor guaranteed. Tell him."

"Yes, Carley, please tell me." Brock pleaded from the bedroom door.

Both women looked over at him standing there—one with wary amusement, the other with hesitant expectation.

Brock never took his eyes off Carley as he walked over to the bed. Becca stood, handed the hairbrush to Brock, and offered her parting words. "I think I'd better go and make sure the store is still standing and making a profit. I'll see you guys later—love you, Cars, and remember what I said. Oh—and breathe!"

Both Brock and Carley nodded in acknowledgment of Becca's farewell but never altered their gazes from each other.

Brock sat down behind Carley, took up the hairbrush, and continued brushing her hair where Becca left off. He took great pleasure in gently stroking the brush through her beautiful, naturally strawberry blonde curls. When he stopped, Carley turned her head toward him, anticipation shining brightly in her eyes.

"I do, you know. I do love you. I have since a day not too long after I moved into my condo."

"That day, I had been rushing off to the bookstore, running late as usual, and when I stepped outside, the sight of you chasing a helium balloon for that little girl took my breath away. You were so powerfully persistent in your pursuit of a Dora the Explorer helium balloon, and yet so gentle with that child when you couldn't get her balloon back. You had her laughing about something when you and her mother calmed her down."

"I was very late for story hour that day, but it was all worth facing Becca's impatience. I never found out whether you knew them or not, but I want you to know that they came into the bookstore later that day, and I made sure the book *Where Do Balloons Go?* made it into their shopping bag. I've always hoped it would make her happy. I've never seen them again. I guess they were tourists."

Brock pulled her around to face him. "I know the timing is not the best, Carley Leigh Lyons, but I love you too. And do you want to know when the first time was that you came to my attention in that wonderfully fated kind of way?"

"Yes," Carley breathed heavily as their lips touched for the first time.

With his lips still close to hers, Brock told her the story of the first time she caught his attention, as they discovered how God's lifespan tapestry wove their lives from the very beginning.

"Yes, they were tourists," he said, "but not ordinary tourists. That little girl is named Cassidy, and her mother's name is Samantha Hogan-Smythe. They are Bryan's sister and niece. They were in town to take Cassie to Lewiston Children's Hospital for her first of many chemo appointments. The balloon was for comfort, to make her smile a little bit, and—as you saw—when she accidentally lost it, she was heartbroken. They were in your store on my recommendation. I had seen you watching us and immediately thought to substitute a *Dora the Explorer* book for the lost balloon. Imagine Sam's surprise when they got to the hospital and found another book in her bag. A book she had not paid for—yet inexplicably about helium balloons. Sam still thinks an angel was watching out for her daughter and placed the book there. I was positive you had done that wonderful, caring act of random blessing, and now I can tell her that was exactly what happened. Lord knows how I love you, Carley."

Carley kissed him back, then paused to ask, "Is she okay now?"

"Cassidy?" Brock asked between kisses. "Yes. She went into remission and remains there today. She's outgrown her fascination with *Dora*, but still loves balloons of all types. I think you might have started an obsession for her. She 'collects' balloons now, so for her last birthday, I sent her on a balloon ride for an hour with a picnic lunch with her mom and dad at the end of it. She was thrilled."

Carley kissed him long and hard. Brock groaned as he gently cradled her face and kissed her back with a tender fire currently rivaling a brush fire through his body—lighting them both up like a beacon of hope for all their tomorrows.

Brock stroked his tongue across her lips, and she instantly opened her mouth to his quest, deep in her passion for his probing tongue. As he moved his hands down her back, he pulled her even closer to him. Carley groaned in both pleasure and pain as several of her incisions protested violently to being stretched to capacity.

Brock immediately loosened his grip and started apologizing. "Carley, Sweetheart, I'm so very sorry—here, let me help you sit."

Carley leaned in and kissed him quiet. "I've been dying for your kiss for a very long time, Brock. Be quiet and do it some more," she demanded as she moved carefully further into his embrace.

Brock swung her legs out from under her with little effort and no interruption in their kissing and walked over to the lounge chair in the corner of the bedroom. He sat with her in his lap and continued kissing her mouth without pain.

"On the other hand," Brock murmured, "little Miss Innocence, can you let this be enough for now—making out with your boyfriend?"

"As your newly appointed girlfriend," she continued, "I fully intend to kiss you as much as possible, as long as Dr. H didn't forbid it."

Brock countered, "He didn't warn me at all. And he knew you were coming home with me to stay. He definitely knew what I feel for you—and he still didn't say anything about abstinence from kissing."

"I'm excited beyond belief to finally be tasting your kisses and feeling the warm embrace of your arms around me. I've finally found my way to you—and even if it did take an act of violence, that will have to be the good to come from it and take away its power, if I ever remember it."

"Sweetheart, I don't know if I can continue this way with you right now. Except I've been waiting so long that I cannot seem to stop. You absolutely take my breath away—and I don't seem to want it back." Brock punctuated each word with a kiss as he continued. "Please always know that I will treasure you beyond all that is, was, and will be. You will always be safe with me. Always."

With tears spilling freely down her cheeks, Carley kissed Brock again. "I love you, Brock. I know you will never hurt me. I will do my best to never hurt you either. But I cannot remember the attack. I hope I never do."

Brock knew what temptations could beset them if they didn't take this conversation out of the bedroom. So he picked Carley up in his arms to carry her out.

Carley was indignant. "Wait—what are you doing, Brock? Where are we going?" she pouted sweetly.

Brock stopped abruptly in the central hall, looked down, kissed her gently, and answered, "I cannot, in good conscience, continue to have this conversation in the bedroom, Sweetheart. You've already stated your desire to wait for your wedding night to honor God's Word. I happen to concur. And that being said, you need more time to heal, and I need less temptation to defile you myself—healing wounds notwithstanding."

There was so much love in his eyes and words that Carley could only gasp. Then, with a self-satisfied smile, she cuddled further into his arms. "Alright then," she breathed against his neck, "carry on."

Brock moaned low in his throat, enjoying the attention Carley was bestowing on his neck. "You really play unfair, Sweetheart. Okay, cheater, we're going to have to go up to the roof garden to keep both of us in God's will." He added, with a half-laugh, "We also may need to rethink me being available after you take your pain medication."

He made a hard right and strode straight for the spiral staircase made of ornate cherry wood and wrought iron that led to his private rooftop garden.

At the top of the stairs, they encountered the door.

"Sweetheart," Brock requested, "would you please punch the code into the keypad for me?"

"Me?" Carley asked in surprise. "You want me to know the code to your condo?"

Brock smiled the smile of a self-satisfied Cheshire cat. "Of course. It's now your home also. And in the interest of full disclosure, I don't rent this penthouse—I own it."

"What? W.I.L.D. let you buy your condo?" Carley protested with a suppressed giggle.

At Brock's inquiring eyebrow lift, Carley elaborated, "I've always gotten a huge giggle out of a company named W.I.L.D." She giggled again, then pulled herself up short. "Wait. What? My home also? What exactly do you mean by that?"

Brock's Cheshire grin was replaced with a mixture of amusement and confusion, but he only responded, "Three-seven-eight-nine-two, pound sign, if you don't mind."

Carley grinned devilishly as she complied with his request. "Right, sir. Yes, sir. Entering three-seven-eight-nine-two, pound sign. Entered as ordered, sir. Please don't punish me, sir."

"Minx," Brock muttered as he turned the handle, opened the door, and carried her to one of the two elegant lounge chairs on the far side of the garden.

The potted tree sitting between the two loungers was still holding onto its final autumn leaves and made a stunning foreground to the tail end of the fall annuals still struggling to survive in the increasingly cold Lewiston autumn. The button mums, chrysanthemums, hardy roses, and phlox ground cover made the garden a place of stunning beauty. Even with the water feature shut down for the winter, its river rock composition didn't in any way detract from the peaceful design of Brock's rooftop sanctuary.

In the corner opposite her, Carley saw something that confused her. It looked like a covered triangular birdcage fitted into the corner behind the patio set, but before she could ask Brock about it, he continued.

"You make me crazy with your mouth in so many ways, you know that, right? You may need a spanking." The tenderness with which he deposited her onto the lounge chair belied his threat... she hoped.

Brock eyed her with consternation as he continued, "To answer your first question—yes. Your home also. Right now, out of necessary security. But trust me when I tell you, we will be discussing long-term arrangements before very much longer. I can no longer live without you in my life daily, which answers your second question."

"Now, as to W.I.L.D.," he looked at her askance, "what in the world makes you giggle yourself silly about that?"

"Oh, well, umm," a tiny giggle escaped her, "you're going to think I'm a little insane when I tell you this, but every time I think about it—especially when I write out my rent check each month—I imagine Mrs. Bruns and Ken having a 1960s-era disco dance party in the basement to celebrate. I don't know why, it just is. I was planning to put it in a book one day..." She giggled again.

Brock stared at her with his mouth slightly agape in shock. "Carley," he began, but choked on his own words with a laugh and had to start over.

"Carley, I own W.I.L.D., Incorporated. Which in turn owns many other properties, both residential and industrial—including this building. So now that you know that, who do you picture in your little disco fantasy, hmm?"

"Personally, I now see you in a gorgeous mini skirt and me in a John Travolta suit, dancing to 'Stayin' Alive' and getting all hot and sweaty on the dance floor... and having the time of our life—on and off the dance floor."

Then in the next heartbeat, Carley sputtered in shock. "You own this building? W.I.L.D., Incorporated? Whe n... Geez... dancing, disco, mini skirt—holy moly. Really, Brock? Are you trying to scare me? Is that why your company is named W.I.L.D.?" She looked up at him with real concern, the question plain in her eyes.

Brock let out a full belly laugh. "Slow down, Sweetheart. I just let you know that I am a very wealthy man and all you can ask is if I like disco and you in a mini skirt?"

"Right now, I want to clarify what W.I.L.D. stands for. It means *Westcott Integrity Land Development, Incorporated.* Good Lord, woman, life with you is never going to be boring. I am going to enjoy loving you forever." Brock admitted with a smirk.

"That's going to make Momma a very happy grandmomma, Baby Boy."

The voice from over at the stairway caused Carley to squeak in alarm as she just about climbed up Brock's abruptly turned back.

At Brock's resigned sigh, Carley peeked over his shoulder to see Dani—Brock's sister—pausing at the stairway with a huge smile on her face.

"Dani," he introduced, "please meet Carley Leigh Lyons, the love of my life. Carley, Sweetheart, meet Barbara Danielle Thorne—aka Squirt—my twin sister."

Dani smiled as she walked up to their lounge chair, where Carley was carefully reinstalling herself with Brock's thoughtful help.

"Hello, Carley, it's nice to officially meet you. Please call me Dani. Baby Boy here is my little brother, who knows better than to scoff at my size. I'm at the perfect height to punch the boy right in the most tender man parts. You'd think he'd give a little more care, especially now that future grandchildren are at stake." Dani sent a glare Brock's way as she mock-punched him—quite literally—below the belt.

As Brock judiciously moved out of her reach, Carley replied warmly, "Nice to officially meet you too. We've met a couple of times before today though. I've lived in this building for a little over two years now, so I do know a little about how you two interact. And with that observation, I would appreciate no punching. I'm hoping to not be single too much longer, and I want the man I love there with me on the honeymoon—and fully functional. I was also hoping for at least two children."

She blushed prettily as she looked hesitantly up at Brock, who was nodding earnestly.

"Anything you want, Sweetheart. Anything at all," he affirmed.

Immediately, the blush that graced her face overtook her entire body as she realized what she had just said. She stared helplessly at Brock for help and intervention with her currently overactive mouth and TMI outpourings.

Brock took his cue and interrupted, picking Carley up and settling her into his lap once again.

"Hey, how did you get in here, Squirt? I've changed the codes to all the doors and added additional security measures to the building to keep trouble like you out."

Dani smirked at Brock as a voice answered from the stairway.

"I let her in."

"Geez!" Carley exclaimed in a squeal as Chase's voice startled her. She clutched her chest as Brock held her steady on his lap. She gasped for air, staring owlishly at Dani and Chase, who were now gaping at her in return.

"Wow," Carley apologized. "I'm sorry. I don't usually startle so easily," she lamented as a new blush climbed up her cheeks.

Brock smiled, turned her head, and kissed her—deepening the blush.

"It's okay, Sweetheart. Chase scares all women. Isn't that right, Dani?"

Dani blushed, and Chase cocked an eyebrow at Brock while sending a sidelong glance at Dani, but he refrained from rising to the bait. Instead, he turned fully to Brock and asked, "You wanted to see me?"

Brock turned back to Carley for a moment. "Sweetheart, will you be okay sitting up here with Dani while Chase and I go to the office for a few minutes?"

Carley was staring mutely at the lounge on the other side of the potted tree. Slowly, she turned her face back to Brock with a wide, unblinking stare.

"Umm... no. I don't think Dani or I will be safe up here alone, Brock. I'm certain we would be in more danger here—alone."

An uncertain look on Brock's face was replaced with disbelief when he looked past her and saw what she saw.

He looked sharply at Dani, who was staring, shell-shocked, down at the other lounge.

"What the...?" both Brock and Chase exclaimed together, as they all took in what Carley had already seen—and realized exactly what it was sitting on the other lounge chair.

"Nobody touches those."

Chase immediately went into detective mode, reaching to pull Dani over to him. For once, Dani didn't argue or immediately step away.

"Brock, call Detective Hayes—now!" Chase barked when Brock didn't immediately move from Carley to reach for his phone.

Brock glared at him, then pulled out his cell and made the call.

Chase sat Dani down with Brock and Carley as he pulled on latex gloves from his pocket. After snapping several photos with his cell phone, he carefully lifted the black panties to reveal the entirety of the presumably blood-stained note and the variegated posy of red paper flowers set beneath them.

"What does the note say?" Carley inquired with a slight shake to her voice.

Chase looked at Brock, who mutely nodded. Carley dimly registered this *me man, protect woman* moment but stowed it away for chastisement at a more suitable time.

Chase hesitated, then read,

"Wives and daughters are the man of the family's responsibility to discipline—ALWAYS. Anticipate my protection in your fragile condition, my love."

"What the heck?!" Brock exploded.

"Unfortunately, I think I know," Chase answered grimly, sending Brock a look that Carley knew meant more unexpected anguish for them all.

Chapter 5

What is going on? How has his wife gotten his well-formed plans derailed so swiftly and effectively? At this rate, she will have racked up more punishment than Jessica received.

He didn't mean to actually let her die—but the little witch wouldn't cooperate and take her punishment with dignity. Not as dignified as his wife had.

And just that easily, thoughts of possibly never seeing Carley again send his rage soaring, along with waves of anger and evil that constantly surround him like smoke from a cauldron.

To top it all off, he's sure he saw a face watching his early morning garden invasion. He continued to grumble to himself as he counted windows, then paid a visit to the building behind Westcott to check the mailboxes—to see who may have been watching him.

If I counted correctly, that window belonged to Cindy Grant. Well, that makes things a bit more complicated. Her connection with Bryan makes it more difficult—but it's her connection to Brock that may complicate issues I don't want further complicated. I may have to pay her a visit very soon—tonight, perhaps—to correct another one of Carley's little messes.

If she would just own up to being his, then none of this other ridiculous nonsense would have needed to happen. They could be long gone from here and all would be as it is fated to be.

Nothing here is going to stop him from having her as his own. It's fate—and if she thinks fate is to be thwarted, then she obviously didn't learn her lessons well enough in the closet.

She has no choice, and I'll make sure she regrets it if she decides to leave me again. Regret—with pain so unbearable that she'll wish she were dead.

Carley was sitting at the patio table with Dani and a paramedic, recovering from her panic attack and hyperventilating into an oxygen mask over her mouth. The pill

Brock had shoved down her throat fifteen minutes ago was starting to kick in nicely.

The paramedic, who had introduced herself as Kelly, radioed down to her partner, Dave, on the street, letting him know Carley was refusing transport. "Just bring up an AMA waiver," she told Dave with no small amount of resigned exasperation.

Brock shot Carley a dark look across the roof when he heard Kelly's loud and irritated pronouncement. Carley, however, didn't care. She pulled down her oxygen mask and stuck her tongue out at him before turning away to give her attention to Kelly.

"I just got out of the hospital, and I'm not going back for one teeny-tiny panic attack that you and my medication now have under control."

Kelly placed the oxygen back over Carley's mouth, gently pushed her head between her knees with a glare, and didn't say a word.

Dani leaned over from her own chair and her own paramedic, Jeffrey—"who is totally hot and bothersome," as Dani had informed her earlier—and asked in a whisper, "Those were bloody black panties that smeared the note and the lounge, weren't they?"

"Yeah, that's what it looked like," Carley answered her with as grim a look as her oxygen mask and head between her knees would allow. "I have a very bad feeling they're going to turn out to be mine. They looked like mine."

Kelly and Jeffrey looked up, startled. While getting her history, they had both heard what had happened to her, but this was something altogether different. Kelly, Dani, and Jeffrey all looked at one another in confusion, but Dani asked what was on all their minds.

"How in the blazes would you think—or know—something like that?"

Carley sighed heavily. "Yeah... unfortunately, that was one of the pieces of clothing not recovered at my own... umm... crime scene. And they really look like the pair I was wearing that day." Carley sighed significantly again and leaned back in her chair, closing her eyes to all the police and medical chaos—and Brock's glares—swirling like gnats around her.

"And those flowers, you know, those paper ones? I've seen them before, but where?" Carley further mused, drifting in and out of the conversations around her.

"Why don't you go downstairs, Carley," Detective Hayes quietly suggested as she walked over to check on her and Dani. "We're going to be here a while, and I'll come to you when I'm done here. You look all in." Robyn was solicitous, as if talking to a friend. "Go ahead and rest for a while."

Carley opened her eyes and smiled gratefully at Detective Hayes saying, "Thanks, Robyn. I think I would prefer that. Dani, care to join me? I'm going to get silly on my meds real soon, and I can guarantee you a good giggle or two when I do."

Dani and both paramedics all busted out in highly inappropriate laughter, as Robyn stood by, merely smiling, while they all acquiesced to her gracious and slightly against-the-rules invitation.

Kelly helped Carley to her feet, and Jeffrey gallantly offered Dani his arm. They all quickly and carefully made their way back down into Brock's condo.

They met Dave coming up.

"Hey Dave, will you go on up and get my gear, please?" Kelly asked her partner as she and Carley made it the rest of the way down the spiral staircase and into the living room.

"Jeffrey," Dave inquired, "you want me to grab your gear too?"

"Nah," Jeffrey answered. "I grabbed my kit." He held it up to show the truth of his statement—and possibly the strength of his arm—as Dani flirted shamelessly with him.

"You are so strong, Jeffrey. You must work out."

"Sure, I do," he replied nonchalantly. "We all must in order to do our jobs well. Some days it takes pure brawn to lift stretchers all day."

Kelly, Carley, and Dave all barked out a laugh as Kelly taunted him. "Why don't you go pump some iron, dude, and get off Chase's girl before you get seriously beaten."

Carley and Dave laughed outright while Dani spluttered, and Jeffrey backed away cautiously, looking over Dani's shoulder to see Chase staring at him with just a hint of menace in his eyes.

"Yes, Jeffrey," Chase agreed mildly, "go somewhere else and pump some iron."

Dani spluttered some more. "For goodness' sake, Chase, you don't own me—my time, let alone my body. I'll flirt with whomever I choose," she declared self-righteously.

Silence descended over the room as Jeffrey made a quick exit. All except for Carley's ill-suppressed, apparently drug-induced giggling.

Everyone ignored her, all eyes on Chase and Dani as they faced each other defiantly.

Just as quickly, Chase took a step back and grinned as he responded, "Barbara Danielle Thorne, that is not what you told me yesterday. Several times too, *Precious One*, as I recall."

Dani started sputtering again, and Carley outright belly-laughed as Chase turned his back and strode right back up the stairs into Brock's half-angry, half-amused countenance.

"I cannot go back down there right now, dude," Chase told Brock. "I've gone and pissed Her Royal Highness off again."

"You had better not just be playing with my sister, friend, or I'll have to maim you and feed you to Carley's squirrels," Brock coolly informed him.

Chase gave Brock an equally quelling glare. "You can try, dude—but it's not me who's playing games with others' hearts here, my friend."

Brock stared into the steady blue eyes of his best friend and nodded, then stepped back and let Chase precede him back onto the roof.

"I still need to talk to you in private, Chase. And soon," Brock reiterated.

"Yeah, I know. But apparently, it's going to have to wait a little while. I think the other princess up here needs our attention right now." Chase indicated Detective Hayes with a slight nod in her direction.

Brock turned to fully face Detective Hayes, looked her in the eyes, held out his hand to shake hers, and asked, "How's it coming along, Detective?"

Robyn removed her glove and took Brock's hand in hers, replying, "Just fine, thanks. The CSU team is wrapping up and will be leaving shortly. I, however, need to stay and interview the four of you."

"I supposed as much," Brock responded. "Shall we go downstairs with everyone else?"

"After you, Detective." Brock held out his hand, inviting Robyn to the staircase.

"Thank you, Mr. Thorne," Robyn responded as she started down the stairs.

"I think I'll stay up here and make sure CSU finishes up," Chase offered. "I can give you my full statement again officially when you get done downstairs."

Brock and Robyn both smirked knowingly as they headed down the stairs.

"No problem. Thanks, Chase," Robyn replied with distinct laughter in her voice.

When they got to the bottom of the stairs, Brock indicated to his right. "I believe I hear everyone in the living room. After you, Detective."

Robyn turned to her right, passing what was presumably the guest bathroom, and found a beautifully outfitted living room divided from the dining room by an intricately hand-carved Chinese—or maybe Japanese—screen.

Very beautiful, she thought to herself, *and most probably cost the equivalent of my monthly salary. But still... very beautiful.*

There was no pause in her walk or manner as she noticed the screen—her professionalism firmly in place. She stopped only when she saw that two of the paramedics were still there, treating both Dani and Carley.

"Did something else happen?" she asked, a sinking feeling starting to settle in.

Kelly looked up from where she was kneeling by the couch at Carley's head, placing the oxygen mask back over her mouth before rolling up a large afghan that hung over the couch to place under Carley's feet to elevate them. "Yep," she answered, placing a stethoscope in her ears.

Dani sat pale and shaking in an overstuffed chair that seemed to be dragging her ominously into its depths, while Dave took her pulse, lifted her feet onto the ottoman, then began checking her blood pressure. He also pulled another crocheted afghan—one Brock and Dani's mom had made—over her.

Brock backed up briefly to the bottom of the staircase and yelled up, "Chase! Down here. Now!"

Then he stood over both his girls and stared helplessly at them, and then at the two paramedics.

Dave sighed when Kelly refused to answer Detective Hayes' question more fully. "Is your radio not on or something?" he asked Robyn.

"It's in my car," she replied, a bit defensively. "Central knows to call me on my cell if they need me."

Just as she finished speaking, her phone began to ring. She glanced speculatively at the number on her screen and then back up at Dave in surprise as she answered.

"Hayes," she cut out sharply. Listening for a moment, she looked up to see all of them staring at her with varying levels of speculation.

"Oh crap," she whispered. "I'll be right there."

"Wait one minute!" Brock started in, his voice edged with alarm.

But Chase strode in, waving at Brock to quiet down, as he crossed to Dani, tucked his phone between his ear and shoulder, picked her up, and sat back down with her snuggled into his lap.

He ended his call, looked at Robyn, and told her, "Go. I'll fill them in, and we'll all be right here waiting for you when you're done. The coroner is waiting on you."

Everyone turned as they heard what sounded like a herd of ostriches squawking and flapping as the CSU team streamed down the stairs—radios blaring, windbreakers flapping—as they made directly for the front door, their kits in hand.

Robyn just nodded her head at Chase and turned to follow the CSU team out the front door.

Brock strode to the door, shut it, locked it, and re-set the alarm. Then he turned back around and walked into the living room, relieved to see that Carley was conscious again—though she looked decidedly frightened. She silently held out her hand to him, and he immediately made his way to her, while Kelly adjusted herself and her equipment to accommodate him.

Looking at Brock, Kelly filled him in on Carley's condition. "She passed out when the news came across our radios—but only for a few moments. I was able to bring her around without using smelling salts. Also, Dani told me about Dr. Holthouser. I called him at home and he's on alert if needed."

"She"—Kelly cut her eyes to Carley with ill-disguised irritation—"refused to meet him at the hospital. I filled him in on the situation, and he seems to think she'll be fine, but told me to call if anything in her condition changes for the worse."

Brock could hold it in no longer. "What in the blue blazes has happened now?" he demanded.

Carley laid a hand on his chest to soothe him as she answered softly. "Well... Jessica Hines has been found murdered. Umm... in the back lot here. Apparently, in her car. That's... that's all I know."

Brock rubbed Carley's back as he let the news process for a while. He had just discovered he had an employee murdered on the property less than a month after a tenant—Carley—was attacked in his building.

He continued to hold Carley tightly, rubbing her back as if his very life depended on her staying in his arms—and in his life. It probably did.

He looked over at Chase, who was still holding Dani, and asked her gently, "How are you doing, Squirt?"

"I'll be alright," she sighed. "But what about you, Baby Boy?"

Chase and Brock both grinned at Dani's customary response to being called "Squirt," then turned serious again as Kelly spoke.

"Jeffrey and Tonka were called to the scene about 15 minutes ago," she supplied. "They were told not to run sirens. Apparently, dispatch didn't realize they were already here. I assume the parking lot is a different address?"

"You assume correctly," Brock replied. "I purchased the mirror lot behind this building, so the technical address is the street behind. Being on the corner, I had alleyway access put in when I rehabbed the building so the employees could cross the alley and access their respective doors—one to The Laundry and one to The Gym. It's also for tenants to access the side alley and reach the front of the building. It's well-lit. Never saw it as a danger... until now."

Being quiet and respectful of Brock's pain over this terrible news, everyone turned to Chase for more details. Chase looked questioningly at Carley, then Brock. When they both nodded consent, he began.

"First of all," Chase said, "Emmy tried to call in a missing person report on Jessica late last night. But since she's no longer a minor and was only a couple of hours overdue, no official report was filed. The sergeant on duty did make a note on the blotter when he realized where she worked, and he had her description and plates called out on an unofficial BOLO to all patrol cars—to cover his bases, he said."

Chase's tone turned bitter. "As you already know, she was murdered. So that did no end of good."

Dani rubbed his arm and the part of his chest she could reach. Chase calmed down enough to continue.

"She was discovered in her car about"—he checked his watch—"forty minutes ago by Emmy and Bryan."

"Emmy and Bryan?" Brock questioned.

"Yeah," Chase sighed. "From what I currently understand, when Bryan came into The Gym to take over for Emmy, she was panicking and asked if he'd seen Jessica. Bryan told her he hadn't, but that he had seen her car out of his kitchen window earlier today."

Chase paused several nerve-racking minutes to gather his thoughts, then continued.

"Apparently, they walked over to The Laundry first, thinking Jessica must've come straight to work after being out all night—but no. Thomas hadn't seen her since he left yesterday at around three in the afternoon. He tried calling her a few times but only got her voicemail. He was fairly angry, according to Bryan. Apparently, he's been overwhelmed in The Laundry today—with Doris on vacation and Jessica no-showing or calling in, he was covering the desk and trying to do the laundry too. When Bryan told him her car was in the back lot, he came unglued."

Chase shook his head, his voice laced with disbelief. "Thomas told Bryan, and I quote: 'I don't care if she's in pain and without remedy, drag her in hungover by her hair now if you have to. She has customers to deal with so I can get to the laundry—or else she's fired.'"

Chase smirked at Brock's expression and tone. "Like he has that kind of authority. We'll be discussing that."

"Really?" Chase muttered, "That's what you choose to focus on? ...Never mind."

"Anyway," he continued, "when they got within five feet of the car, Bryan hauled Emmy back and called 911. Then he tried calming her enough to stop her from breaking into the car. She kept trying to get in and 'help' Jessica.

I'm told Jeffrey and Tonka had to sedate her when they got there—she wouldn't calm down otherwise. They've already taken her to the hospital. I'm waiting on a call from either Bryan or Hayes with more info."

Dani sighed and sat up. "You can go down if you're needed. I don't want you to get into any trouble because of me."

Chase pulled her back into his warm embrace. "Not my case, *Precious One*, and I've got nowhere else to be. Still have to be questioned by Robyn, remember?"

Dani sighed and snuggled back into Chase's lap, closing her eyes. "Okay," she mumbled.

Carley peeked up at Brock, who gave her a wink and a smile that promised they'd discuss the Chase-and-Dani saga later.

Noticing the sweet interactions on both sides of the room, Kelly and Dave exchanged a glance and began packing their kits. Kelly informed them, "You guys are okay. We're going to get out of your hair. If you need us again, Chase, just call my cell and we'll let dispatch know. Don't forget—Dr. H is on standby too, just in case."

"Just in case of what?" Carley questioned with a giggle.

Brock grimaced, looking at Chase—whose smile said he knew exactly what Brock was going through—and helped his friend out.

"Brock, why don't you go and lay Carley down for a rest? She's going to need a clear head for Robyn's questions."

Brock's smile was brief and grateful as he picked Carley up and carried her off to the bedroom.

"Do you want to lay down or sit up?" Brock asked as he looked into Carley's eyes.

Carley looked back at him with equal parts shy and sly. "Depends. Will you stay with me either way? I don't want to be alone or go to sleep yet. And…"

"Yes?" Brock inquired. "You know you can ask me anything at this point."

Carley blushed, pulled up her big-girl panties, and asked in one quick breath, "Willyoukissmeagainplease?"

Brock laughed. "Was that a real question, Sweetheart? Of course I will kiss you. Anytime you like."

He offered her the sweetest kiss Carley had ever experienced. And isn't that just a little bit sad, Carley began lamenting internally—until she realized Brock was just staring at her with bemusement.

Carley giggled, just as a knock came at the bedroom door, startling them both. They had forgotten they weren't alone in the penthouse.

"What?" Brock asked gruffly.

With a smile laced with a smirk that could clearly be heard in his voice, Chase answered, "Robyn is back and would like a word with you two."

"We'll be out in ten minutes," Brock replied curtly. "You and Dani go first. Thanks, Chase."

Brock turned into the closet/bathroom, closing the door on Carley's giggle—and any negative or snide response that may or may not have come from Chase.

Brock and Carley emerged from the bedroom precisely eighteen minutes later. Brock, fresh from his shower and in different clothes, chose to confront the grinning Nosy Nellies sitting at the dining room table.

"What? Do I have something on my face?" Carley asked innocently.

"A whole sentence and no blush," Chase noted with a smile for them both.

"Chase..." Brock began, but Carley interrupted him.

"It's okay, Brock. He's just jealous he wasn't out here kissing with Dani."

"Oh, good grief," Brock moaned. "Robyn, if you want any coherent answers out of Carley, you better get to them. I just gave her another dose of pain medication, and it must be kicking in."

"Speaking of which," Brock continued, "let's move this party into the kitchen. Carley hasn't eaten in quite a while, and I don't want her getting ill because the pain medication irritates her stomach. So—dinner for all."

Brock walked Carley to the kitchen island and helped her up onto the middle stool.

"Dani, Robyn, would you ladies mind flanking her to make sure she doesn't fall out of her seat, please?"

"No, of course not," Dani replied, as Robyn silently placed her notebook on Carley's opposite side and pulled herself up onto her chair.

Chase was just taking the last chair next to Dani when Brock looked at him. "Would you mind getting everyone a drink? The beverage cooler is stocked."

As Chase walked to the side of the island to peruse the beverages, he opened the cooler door and began listing their choices.

"Looks like Mrs. McGinty went shopping today. Okay ladies, we have Coke, Pepsi, Sierra Mist Cranberry, Diet Dr. Pepper Cherry, plain water, sparkling water in orange, pineapple, and lime, beer, wine, and Snapple Peach Tea."

Dani opted for the Diet Dr. Pepper. Robyn asked for water. Brock requested a beer, and Chase joined him.

Chase looked at Carley, who was clearly waiting for something.

"What can I get for you, Carley?"

"Whiskey," Carley slurred.

"Uh—NO," everyone said at once, startling Carley, who tipped precariously to her right where Robyn was already waiting with a steadying hand. Dani joined her, and together they held Carley upright until she found her own balance again.

"Here." Chase handed over a bottle of water just as Brock laid out a platter of freshly cut fruit.

"Mrs. McGinty must have anticipated company this evening with Carley coming home," Brock praised his enterprising housekeeper. "I'll be right back with the tray of roast beef sandwiches and condiments she also prepared. Chase, please grab the plates and utensils. Does anyone want a glass?"

Brock moved into full host mode, and it was all Carley could do not to giggle at him—so she settled for just sitting and staring at her very handsome boyfriend.

Brock glanced at her questioningly and began to fill her plate.

"Drink your water, Carley. I'll have your plate ready in just a second."

Carley just stared back at him and replied, "I hate plain water. If I cannot have a whiskey, then I want some Crystal Light in my water."

She smothered a yawn as she added, "Now please," with one of her infamous eyerolls.

Chase soothed her. "No problem, Carley, let's just see what flavors Mrs. McGinty has laid in."

He opened the top drawer next to the beverage cooler and reeled off about ten different flavors, then asked, "Which one would you like, Carley?"

"How about... hmm... strawberry lemonade?" she asked sweetly, as she stuffed almost a whole kiwi in her mouth.

"Mmm... this is so good, Brock," she said through an absurdly full mouth. "Geez, I didn't know trauma made a person so hungry. Or tired."

Chase set her doctored bottle of water in front of her. She picked it up and upended it, draining the whole bottle with a very unladylike belch tacked on at the end—for giggles.

Everyone else had stopped eating to watch the spectacle that is a hungry and high Carley. Embarrassment was not an option for medicated Carley. She kept on stuffing her face as everyone looked on with emotions ranging from pride (from Chase) to mild embarrassment (from Robyn).

Chase glanced at Brock and noticed the slightly stunned look on his best friend's face and smiled to himself.

"Well finally," he thought, "at least he and I are on the same track with the wife-and-kids thing. Now to get Dani on board with it too."

Chase sighed as he pulled another bottle of water from the cooler and a packet of Crystal Light, making Carley another strawberry lemonade.

Carley smiled her thanks brightly at Chase as she continued to wolf down a roast beef, banana pepper, horseradish, and Provel cheese sandwich.

She turned in her seat, the worst of the hunger wiped from her face, and asked Robyn, "What do you need to ask me?"

Robyn cleared her mouth of pineapple and took a sip of water to buy herself a moment—to decide how and *if* to proceed, considering Carley's inebriated condition.

Finally, she decided honesty would be the name of the game if she wanted to keep Carley's trust—not to mention keeping her clear-headed for questioning and not bogged down in even more confusion. She held up one finger to Carley as if to say "just a sec," then slipped off her stool and walked over to retrieve her messenger bag from the dining room table.

"Are you sure you want to do this right now—right here—while everyone is eating?" she asked. "It can wait a couple more minutes if you'd prefer to finish."

"I'm done, I think," Carley replied, pushing away her mostly-eaten sandwich.

"Yeah, me too," Dani added as she also pushed her plate away.

Chase and Brock, who were still eating, just nodded their acknowledgment and kept going so Robyn could proceed.

"Okay," Robyn nodded, delving into her bag. She pulled out an evidence bag containing what Carley assumed were the bloodied panties from the roof garden, handed them over, and asked bluntly, "Are these yours?"

Carley carefully took the evidence bag and studied the panties inside.

"Do you know what size they are?" she asked.

Robyn flipped over the bag to consult the affixed label. "Medium," she replied. "And the brand is the same as the bra we found wrapped around Jessica's neck."

Brock moved around the island to hug Carley while Dani tried to comfort her with words.

"I'm so sorry, Carley," she sympathized.

Carley gulped and grabbed Dani's hand, squeezing it tightly. "Yep. Sometimes life really sucks, doesn't it? Because those are my panties—as far as I can tell."

Carley leaned back into Brock's strong chest. She was sobering up now, as the senselessness of what was happening began to truly sink into her awareness again.

She was still dizzy, lethargic, angry, and so very thirsty, but her mind was clearing. That was both good and bad, depending on your perspective. And right now, Carley's perspective felt like the spinning wheel of fortune at a carnival, never quite stopping, never quite settling.

Brock cleared his throat as he hugged her tighter.

"Even when you *do* manage to keep your dialogue internal," he said, "I can still tell everything you're thinking by your body language and facial expressions."

"Everyone here can read every thought that crosses your face, Sweetheart. And this?" he added, his voice firmer. "This is in *no way* your responsibility. You could not have altered the events of the last few days—let alone weeks. Only the sicko doing this could have. So stop. Right now."

Carley sighed and stuck her tongue out at Brock, which included everyone else in the room in her non-verbal protest.

"Fine," she acquiesced. "I know in my head that none of this is my fault, but my heart is hemorrhaging blood and tears for Jessica—and they will not be denied."

Robyn held up her hand to forestall both Brock and Dani, using the calm wisdom of someone who lives this kind of nightmare nearly every day.

"Carley," she said gently but firmly, "you have zero control over other people—especially psychopaths. You can only control your own actions, words, and emotions. If you make this about *you*, you play right into *his* game. You take away what little dignity Jessica has left in her death. And trust me when I tell you—there's precious little dignity in any violent death. Only in the way you conduct yourself after it happens."

"This death may be *connected* to you," Robyn continued, "but it is *not* about you. Jessica crossed his path somewhere—and that's what got her killed. Not you. Not bad luck. Not something you said or did. It's because *he* is a pure psychopath, and he believes everything is about *him*—his wants, needs, and pleasures. Nothing more."

"Three weeks ago, it *was* about you. Now? You need to concentrate on *healing*—both emotionally and physically. Jessica is gone. She no longer has to deal with anything. That's tragically sad. But now it's her Heavenly Father's turn to care for her and lift the weight of her pain and scars—not you. Let Him do that, okay?"

Robyn paused and took a breath. "I can't remember where I heard this, but I think you need to hear it: *'Every scar tells a story.'* Let your scars tell *your* story. Let Jessica's tell hers. We can mourn her life, but we cannot carry her scars. Only the One who bore them all for us can do that."

She looked straight into Carley's eyes.

"I'm done now. Sorry if I offended you. But you need to concentrate on what you *can* do—not what you can't. Alright?"

"Wow," Chase breathed out slowly. "I think that's the most I've ever heard you say at once, Hayes. And may I say—well said. *Very* well said."

Carley and Dani were crying now, and Brock looked suspiciously close to tears himself as he rocked Carley gently in his arms.

Chase moved behind Dani, and she turned in her stool to bury her face in his chest.

Robyn, a bit more composed now, said softly, "Yeah, well... I still have a lot of work ahead of me tonight. So, if you all don't mind, I'd like to finish Brock and Carley's interviews. If you're ready, that is. Then we can all get some much-needed sleep."

There was a slight twinkle in her eyes directed solely at Brock, who returned it with a smile and his full attention as she flipped open her notebook again.

"Okay," she began, "can you start from when you went up to the roof garden with what you remember? I'll interrupt if I need clarification. I have several points I'd like to get your view on from my interview with Chase and Dani."

Brock and Carley carefully walked through their memory of arriving on the rooftop, the casual banter, and the moment things took a dark turn. When they reached the part where the note and panties were discovered, Robyn paused them.

"So, who was the first person to actually notice the note and the panties?" she asked.

Carley answered without hesitation. "I was."

"Okay," Robyn made a note, "what made you notice them when no one else did?"

"Well," Carley began, glancing sheepishly at Brock, "I was sitting on Brock's lap, facing that direction, when I thought I saw someone peeking over the privacy hedge—the one that separates the garden from the utilities and AC units, right behind the water feature."

Robyn frowned in confusion. "Carley, that hedge is about ten feet tall—on top of a three-story building—with the only access through Brock's penthouse. Why do you think you saw someone?"

Carley winced a little at the question, then cleared her throat. "Umm, because I've... maybe... snuck up there a few times in the past using the fire escape. It's not hard. And I've had to hide behind that trellis once or twice myself to wait until the coast was clear. I've done it a bunch of times."

She giggled sheepishly, then added, "I'm sorry, Brock, but I love your garden. When you weren't home, I... borrowed it. I can climb out of my bedroom window, shimmy over to the ladder, and voilà—I'm in paradise."

Brock visibly blanched. "You will *never* do that again. This is now your home, and you will use the spiral staircase like a civilized human being. I'm having that ladder gated and locked immediately. If *you* could do it, someone else could too. Not acceptable."

Robyn, slipping back into official mode, jumped in before the conversation got too personal. "Was it a man or a woman you saw? Did you get a good enough look to describe them?"

Carley shook her head slowly. "No. It was just a flicker—almost a shadow. But I *think* it was female. It was so quick. And I'm on pain meds constantly. I'm not even sure if it was real. I just mentioned it to explain why I turned my head that way and saw the lounge chair."

Robyn nodded, jotting something down in her notebook. "Understood. Let's go through the timeline one more time, just to make sure we have it all straight..."

Carley sighed, but then her eyes widened. She straightened suddenly, gripping the edge of the island.

"We can do that again if you want," she said breathlessly, "but... I *remember* where I've seen those paper flowers before..."

Chapter 6

October 7

Amnesia? No wonder my attempts to catch up with my wife have gotten me nowhere. That must be the reason she holed up with that rich ass Brock. He seems to take his 'responsibilities' way too seriously. I wonder if Carley knows yet that Brock owns this building and that he has a lot to answer for?

She hasn't abandoned me. She just doesn't remember me. Yet. I know she is much too beautiful a woman, inside and out, to treat me so impersonally on purpose. I'll give serious consideration to forgiving her.

Well, now my task is to clean up that one loose end, and then to get through Brock's new and improved security and help my Carley regain her memory so we can begin our life

together. Maybe another note would trigger her memory.
No, another note is obviously not going to be enough to trigger
her memory of me, so it's going to have to be a face-to-face
meeting. Yes, that will trigger her memory and then we're
home free.

But first, I have one Cindy Grant to deal with. The more I
think about her and analyze the problem, I realize I cannot
let Cindy have any power over me. There is just too much else
at stake since that stupid witch Jessica up and died on me.
That really does increase all unwanted exposure. Exposure I
cannot afford, compounded with Carley's amnesia problem.
The only logical solution is a more permanent one.

For the first time, I'm not sure what to do. I hate it
when stupid women complicate my well-ordered life. Cindy
has become Brock's legacy problem. I'm not even sure Brock
knows how much she watches him from her apartment across
the street. Well, there's no other way around it. She made me
her problem and now she is going to regret it. Ready or not,
Cindy Grant... here I come.

Carley woke slowly with a feeling of security and
warmth—not her norm. She stretched carefully and
caught her breath as the pain of healing muscles and ten-
dons reminded her of their slow recovery. It was a healing

pain, though, and that made it bearable. Well, that and Brock. He made everything in her life bearable and worthwhile.

"Good morning, Sweetheart," Brock lightheartedly offered from the door. "Did you sleep well?"

Carley let out a small groan as she carefully rolled to her other side to face him.

"Sweetheart, do you need your pain medication?" Brock's concern was palpable.

"No, I'm just a little bit sore."

Carley grinned mischievously up at him. "I'd rather you be a little less of a chivalrous man—with your lips on mine this morning, if you don't mind."

"Come here," he growled, grabbing her with a gentleness that spoke of great love and care as he kissed her awake.

An hour later and fresh from their respective showers, the doorbell rang. Carley headed for the door, but Brock held her up with a quiet, "Wait." He walked into the kitchen and opened a cabinet on the left wall, checking the display to see Ken Harms, the building maintenance man, standing on their landing looking decidedly nervous and forlorn. Brock quietly waved Carley to a seat in the kitchen and went to answer the door. Carley sat quietly and waited to see what Ken wanted with Brock.

Brock opened the door but stood there, blocking the entrance. He smiled at Ken and asked, "What can I do for you, Ken?"

"Well, sir," Ken swallowed nervously, "Mrs. Bruns sent me up because Detective Braddock has been trying to reach you, and you haven't been answering your phone. So, you know... it's just that Mr. Chase needs to speak with you."

"Thank you, Ken. I'll check my phone and call Chase back right away," Brock responded.

When Ken eyed him even more nervously and didn't move or respond, Brock prompted him again. "Is there anything else, Ken?"

"Well, sir, it's been almost three weeks, like... and, well, I was just wondering if I could see Ms. Carley for a few minutes. It would help ease my nightmares. I think if I could just see her for myself—that she really is okay, you know?"

Brock had decided it wasn't worth the risk and was about to give Ken an apologetic "No" when Carley came around the corner.

"Ken!" she exclaimed, edging past Brock and hugging the man who'd saved her life. "Ken, thank you so much for finding me and getting help so quickly. I guess we both know what would have happened if you hadn't found me in time."

Ken blushed as Carley pulled him in for another hug. "Thank you," she repeated, "thank you so much."

Brock held his tongue and instead held out his own hand. "Carley's right, and I've been remiss in not acknowledging your timely rescue. Thank you, Ken. Thank you for saving the life of my future bride."

Ken looked startled, open-mouthed, and at a loss for anything to say.

Carley carefully pulled back from Ken and nudged her elbow a tad forcefully into Brock's ribs. She held out her left hand for Ken's inspection. "I'm not officially a bride yet, but very soon," she told Ken, beaming rays of sunshine upon him in her happiness.

Ken finally found his voice and started immediately with his congratulations and exclamations of joy for Carley's engagement and recovery.

After accepting Ken's congratulations and agreeing with him on the remarkable progress she had made in her healing, Brock excused himself. Deciding Ken wasn't a threat to Carley's well-being, Brock went in search of his cell phone as they got caught up on each other's lives and commiserated over Jessica's untimely and ugly death.

Brock found his phone in his office on the charger, noting the eighteen missed calls. His hand automatically dialed Chase. He moved back through his office into the bedroom to stand by the door to keep at least one eye on Carley—no matter how unlikely Ken's guilt.

Chase answered on the second ring and growled at Brock, "Found your stalker, dude—and she's dead."

"What stalker, Chase? And dead? What's going on?" Brock struggled to catch up.

"Your love letter writer, unfortunately—and quite by chance." Chase's sigh blew through the line, full of pent-up frustration.

"Chase, can you please start from the beginning?" Brock's own simmering frustration blew back down the line.

"Dude, I'm just across the street, at number 409—the Skyler Building. Why don't you join Robyn and me, and we'll fill you in?"

Chase hung up.

Just as Brock turned back toward his office to look out the right-facing windows at 409 Adams Street, he felt Carley touch his arm. Turning, he found her looking at him with a question in her eyes. A quick glance over her shoulder confirmed Ken had left.

Brock brusquely strode over to reset the alarm and make sure the door was locked before turning back to Carley and grabbing her hand. "There's been another death. I don't know who yet—or even if it's a murder, for that matter—but it's across the street. I'm not sure how it could be related, but Chase rather rudely demanded my presence. Do you know anyone who lives in the Skyler Building?"

"Well," Carley thought, "yes—I do know some people who live there, but none that are good friends or even good acquaintances. In fact, the only tenants I know are customers at the store."

"Okay. Probably not related then, but Chase wants me over there ASAP. I'm going to call Dani and Becca to come stay with you. I'll also let Bryan, Ken, Thomas, and Mrs. Bruns know to be on the lookout for any suspicious people trying to sneak up the stairs."

Brock was in complete go-mode as he pressed the appropriate speed dial number for his sister.

"Hello—" Dani began, but Brock interrupted her.

"Can you come over immediately? Carley will explain when you get here."

"I'm just downstairs—I'll be right up," Dani replied, hanging up quickly.

Brock then speed-dialed Becca.

"Hey Becca, can you come over here ASAP to stay with Carley? She'll explain when you get here."

"Well, since you asked so nicely—sure. I'll be there in about fifteen minutes," Becca replied, and she too hung up on Brock.

Brock turned back to Carley, pulling her into his arms and kissing her soundly before offering a quick tutorial on the penthouse's security systems.

"The front door code is your middle name—L-E-I-G-H and the pound key. The code to the rooftop door is the same as it was yesterday—3-7-8-9-2 and pound. But please don't go up there while I'm gone. I haven't had time to get the locked gate installed over the fire escape ladder yet. Okay, Sweetheart?"

"Of course, Brock. I'm not some simpering foolish girl or overzealous woman who thinks she can take care of everything. I know to be extra careful and not do anything silly or thoughtless that would take me away from you. Not now that I have you."

Brock kissed her soundly again just as Dani fairly shouted through the door while knocking, "It's me! Let me in!"

Brock reluctantly let go of Carley and opened the door for his twin, giving her a quick hug and a "Thank you."

He grabbed his jacket from the hall tree, pocketing his wallet and keys from the bowl on the hall table. As he turned toward the door, he gave Dani some last-minute instructions.

"Make sure Carley eats. There are plenty of leftovers in the kitchen. And please show her the panic room and explain how it works. You might want to wait for Becca—she should know what to do too. Carley will fill you in on what we know so far, which isn't much. And I'll call as soon as I have more information. Oh—and we're engaged. Carley can fill in those gaps too."

Brock smiled at his sister's open mouth as he let himself out of the penthouse. "I love you both very much. Be safe. And don't forget to lock the door and key the code after me."

With that final admonishment, Brock shut the door, and the snick of the latch echoed in the stunned silence pervading the hall.

Dani pulled herself out of her shock, checked the lock, and rearmed the alarm before turning to Carley and asking, "Engaged? Already? Baby Boy sure moves fast."

Carley looked at her warily until Dani smiled. "Mom and Dad will be overjoyed! Congratulations, Carley. I'm going to love having you for a sister." Dani hugged her, both of them shedding happy, familiar girl-tears.

Carley hugged her back, smiling through her own tears. "It's going to be great to have a sister. I've been alone for a long time—well, except for Becca—but she's more like that crazy cousin you only acknowledge at family reunions and holidays."

They both giggled before shifting back to serious business.

"So... a panic room?" Carley asked. "Where in the world is there room for a panic room in this penthouse? All the space is used so effectively. Bedroom with adjacent office, kitchen with dining room, and a living room—I see no space for it."

Dani smiled. "Let's wait for Becca so I only have to explain it once. Besides, Brock said you need to eat. Let's do that while we wait for her. I'd also love to know what's going on across the street—but that can wait on Becca too. Let's eat... and celebrate that gorgeous rock on your finger. Wow! When did you two go out and pick it out?"

"Go? Seriously?" Carley asked incredulously. "I don't think Brock is going to let me out of this penthouse until Mr. Psycho is caught. No, he had it already. Now that you mention it, I have no idea when he bought it, but I love it. I would've probably picked something much smaller though. But I love it—and I very much love your brother."

They made lunch from the leftovers in companionable silence, both waiting patiently for Becca to arrive.

Dani took a bite of her sandwich and waved a hand at Carley to do the same before chewing and responding, "I can see that, Carley. It makes my heart glad for you both. I'm glad Baby Boy found you—and vice-versa. But in all seriousness, I'm thrilled... and a little jealous of you both too."

Carley looked sideways at Dani as she chewed. Swallowing, she asked gently, "I thought you and Chase might be tying the knot very soon. It's obvious you love each other deeply."

Before either could say more, a knock came at the door.

Dani breathed a sigh of relief and turned to check the video display in the cabinet. She stared at the screen, confused and somewhat stunned by the sight: a woman dressed in bold Halloween colors, sporting shockingly black hair with two white stripes zig-zagging upward like a Marge Simpson-Bride of Frankenstein hybrid.

Dani turned to Carley only to find her striding toward the door.

"Wait—Carley—" Dani started, but Carley already had the door open and was being enveloped in what she sincerely hoped was a hug and not an attack.

The two women embraced before Carley shut the door, re-entered the code, and turned to Dani. "Dani, this is

Becca Love. I thought you two had met before—on several occasions, no?"

"Of course," Dani exclaimed. "Yes, I... we have met. Umm... I've just never met *Marge Frankenstein* before... Uh... how are you, Becca?"

Becca laughed. "Doing good. And you?"

"Other than being a bit confused—I'm doing good, also." Dani's bewilderment still sat plainly on her face.

Carley and Becca chuckled together.

"What book are you reading now?" Carley asked, taking Becca's coat and hanging it on the coat tree, revealing a very unusual dress and black platform boots.

A lightbulb seemed to go off over Dani's head.

"Children's Book Club Reading Hour—right. I remember now. Wow. I guess I never realized just how *all-out* you guys go for that. So... what are you reading to the rugrats now?"

"We're reading *Dr. Frankenstein's Other Monster,*" Becca said with a grin. "And they're more the age of *unholy terrors.* Rugrats are on Wednesday mornings."

"Right," Dani acknowledged with an answering grin and the dawning of a new friendship.

"So," Becca got straight to the point. "Who's going to tell me what the heck is going on now? I saw the CSU squad cars and crew outside across the street. So—who died now?"

"Well…" Dani said, glancing at Carley, who nodded that she should continue. "Can we walk and talk? Brock asked me to show you both how to access and use the panic room."

"Panic room?" Becca smirked. But when she saw Dani's serious expression, her tone changed. "Oh—you're serious. Sorry. I thought you were joking to get a laugh."

"Nope," Dani replied dryly. "Brock's been preparing for his Carley for a while now. The ring and panic room are just a few items on the Carley checklist he checked off today. The wedding will be next, I suspect."

"Geez," Carley looked pale and stunned. "Just how long has he been planning our life together?"

"Well…" Dani backtracked, "don't flip out, okay? He's just such an anal-retentive, Type A, list-making fanatic that I think he started your very, *very* subtle seduction soon after you moved in."

Carley gaped at Dani as she followed her through the bedroom into Brock's office. "That was over two years ago," Carley said in amazement. "Why in the world hasn't he said anything until now?"

"Good grief! Am I the last to know about this?" Becca complained.

"Nope. The third," Carley said with a smile. "Brock told Ken and Dani. You are my first official notification, though, if it helps."

Dani crouched down to the lower bookshelf just inside the door of the office to activate the panic room lever—and to avoid Carley's questions. She wouldn't want to give away *all* of Brock's secrets after all.

Meanwhile, Becca grabbed Carley's left hand and let out a wolf whistle. "Wow, girl. That is *one* gorgeous setting," Becca gushed. "I'm so jealous. You know, of the ring—not the sappy, silly love crap. Congrats. I'm sincerely happy for you both... despite my jealousy over that ring."
She smiled devilishly. "I wouldn't leave that thing lying around within my reach or you might end up filing an insurance claim."

Before Carley could reply, they both gasped as Dani tripped the lever and a hidden door in the bookshelves opened. Becca and Carley turned toward Dani in astonishment.

"Wow," they said in unison.

Dani smiled. "Yeah, I know—cool, right? This is only the second time I've done this. Come on down, and let me show you how it works." She pushed the door fully open and gestured to a specific shelf. "Feel right here," she instructed Carley, guiding her hand to the spine of a book titled *Odd Apocalypse.* "There are actually three buttons built into this spine. You have to press them in the right sequence the *first* time, or the room won't open again for four hours from this side. I'll show you the other side in a minute."

"I think I've fallen down the white rabbit's hole," Becca muttered.

"Anyway," Dani continued, ignoring the comment, "remember the book is *Odd Apocalypse.*"

"Of course it is," Becca said, still riding her sarcasm wave.

Carley elbowed her in the ribs gently while Dani kept explaining. "It's not a real book. It's the only fake one on a shelf full of Dean Koontz novels. The spine is divided into three segments—each a button. The current code is: bottom, top, top, bottom, top, top, middle. Remember, if you don't get it right on the first try, it locks down for four hours. That's a failsafe in case an intruder finds the lever *and* the fake book. The odds of them guessing the correct code on the first try? Practically zero."

"Don't ever underestimate the odds of Carley's bad luck," Becca cut in again. "It's amazing, really, how much bad karma haunts her every move."

Dani stood up and gave her a dry look. "Not anymore, Becca. Brock won't allow it."

Carley and Becca both laughed, and Carley reassured Dani kindly. "It's okay, Dani. It's just an old worn-out joke. I tend to fall down—and unfortunately *up*—stairs. It's funny because I rented a condo in a walk-up building. It's just an old joke between old friends."

Becca gave Dani a half-apologetic smile. "Sorry. Sometimes I forget not everyone gets my brand of funny. I *do* know this is serious, and I'll stop cracking wise. It's just my fail-safe, you know? But I'll stop—I promise."

Dani softened. "Okay, enough girl drama. I'm sorry too. I can overreact sometimes."

She turned back to the wall of books. "The way I remember the code is thinking of the buttons as numbers. Bottom is 'nine,' top is 'one,' and middle is 'oops.' So the current code would be: 9-1-1-9-1-1-oops. That's how I remember it."

"Clever," Becca admitted.

"Ingenious," Carley agreed. "That'll work for me too. Can I try it this time?"

"Go for it," Dani said with a smile, stepping aside.

***

Brock strode across the street to find the door into the Skyler building barred by a patrolman.

"Sorry, sir," the patrolman explained, "this is an active crime scene and no one is allowed into the building at this time."

"I understand. However, Chase—Detective Braddock—sent for me, Officer Roberts," Brock responded with ill-disguised impatience as he glanced past the patrolman to see Chase leaning over the first-floor railing watching the scene below unfold.

With a grin, Chase yelled from his perch, "Roberts, it's okay to send him up. Just make note of it in the crime scene log."

"Yes, sir." Roberts answered as he moved out of Brock's way and made a note of his arrival and the time on the log sheet for posterity.

Brock took the stairs two at a time to join Chase on the first-floor landing. "What's going on?" he asked bluntly. "Why did you need me to come over here, and what stalker do I have that I'm not aware of, but you are?"

"Whoa, slow down, Brock. I'll get there." Chase's grin died a little. "Do you know Cindy Grant?"

Brock thought for a few moments. "Didn't Bryan date a Cindy Grant for a couple of months about a year ago? I believe she's been to the penthouse with him a few times. That Cindy Grant?"

"Yeah, she's the one—and she was murdered this evening downtown at the corner of Main and South, about four blocks from here. Brock, she was pushed in front of a speeding taxi. It's the fifth fatal 'push and run' we've had here in Lewiston in the last eight months."

"Okay, what does that have to do with me, or with Carley's case? Isn't The Pusher your case? And why is Robyn being pulled from Carley's case to work this one?" Brock asked with mounting anger.

"Calm down, dude," Chase admonished. "Unfortunately, they are related—and you need to see what we found in Ms. Grant's apartment."

At Brock's confused look, Chase explained further. "The responding officer to the push and run took a statement from an eyewitness at the scene that indicated this may be a copycat murder. A murder more related to Carley's attack and Jessica's death. If that's true, we are up to three assaults, two resulting in death—and this guy is escalating at an alarming rate."

Robyn walked down from the second floor just in time to hear the end of Chase's explanation. "Unfortunately, Chase is correct. This is a copycat, and it is related to Carley's case. Chase called me in because of his familiarity with both cases. He recognized the significance of the statement Officer Statler took at the scene and called me ASAP."

"Okay, I believe you. It's connected. But what does having a stalker I didn't know about have anything to do with Carley's attack or anything else related to her case? I still don't see the connection." Brock's impatience was showing in his face and body language as he glared at them both.

Robyn held out her right arm indicating Brock should precede her up the stairs. "I have something I need to show you, and then we can explain everything to you more fully and cohesively. Trust me, Brock, it's very pertinent."

Brock, Chase, and Robyn walked up to the third floor before Chase walked down the hall to the tiny, yet very neat and clean, apartment of Ms. Cindy Grant. They all logged in with the officer at the door and donned gloves and booties as they entered.

Moving into the dining room, there was—spread across every flat surface—reams and reams of written-upon lined paper.

"Was she working on a novel?" Brock asked in confusion.

"No, not quite," Chase answered him. "She was a prolific letter writer, and they are addressed to just one person. You, Brock."

"What?" Brock exclaimed incredulously. "Are you seriously telling me that this Cindy Grant is—or rather, was—'Lady Love'?" Brock was stunned as he looked around. "And all this?" he indicated the mountains of paper everywhere. "These are all more love letters written but not sent to me? Son of a gun."

"Yeah, that about sums it up. By the way, how many letters have you actually received and still have in your possession?" Chase inquired.

"What? Oh," Brock started with a stunned expression at Chase's question, "I'm not exactly sure on the exact number," he mused. "I know there are at least fifty in the office files and at least another hundred or so at home." Brock looked around in abject wonder, tinged with growing shadows of horror. "How many are here?"

"We don't have a complete count yet," Robyn answered him as she slid a look to Chase. "As of right now, we are up to just over 1,300—and we are still finding them everywhere." She hesitated as Brock visibly blanched, but continued at Chase's nod. "Based upon what we are finding in each room—and with four more rooms to go—I'd estimate we'll end up finding about another 4,200 or so."

"Holy crap!" Brock exclaimed.

"According to the dates on the letters," Robyn continued, "and Chase's estimate of when Mr. Hogan started dating Ms. Grant, we think she started writing to you just a couple of weeks before starting her relationship with Mr. Hogan."

"I've got a call into Bryan," Chase clarified, "just to verify our dates and try to get a handle on how she fits into this case. We're hoping Bryan can provide a clue to that end."

"Anyway," Chase continued, "I think we can safely assume that your 'Lady Love, letter stalker' days are over."

"Well, as much as a relief as it is that the love letter writing campaign is over, I still don't see how her tragic death impacts Carley's case." Brock looked around him sadly, not knowing what else to say.

"Well," Chase began, "like I said, one of the witnesses at the scene of Ms. Grant's murder gave a very interesting statement about the man that pushed her into the street. He states that the man was mumbling under his breath in the moments before he shoved his way through the crowd waiting at the corner to cross the street to push Ms. Grant into the street."

Chase paused to collect his thoughts and consult his notes before continuing. "The witness said he was mumbling about how much this was—and I quote—'all Carley's fault and she is in so much trouble.' At first, the witness thought that Cindy was this Carley the man was mumbling about. When he found out she was Cindy, not

Carley, he tried to amend his statement to match the facts. He thought he had misunderstood the perp."

"Oh, my God," Brock muttered in fascinated revulsion.

"However," Chase continued, nodding at Brock in agreement, "Officer Statler was taking the statement and is familiar with both cases. Instead of changing the witness's statement, he called both me and Robyn immediately."

Brock was turning pale as he looked between Robyn and Chase, dread dawning in his face. "Did the witness get a good look at the perp? And why do you think this man is copycatting The Pusher? Why is it not the same person responsible for both sets of murders?"

Chase looked at Robyn, then back to Brock and launched into an explanation. "Well first, Mr. Prosecuting Attorney, we know that The Pusher is a woman. That is not public knowledge. But it has been verified by at least one eyewitness at every Pusher crime scene. Also, The Pusher doesn't mumble curses or anything before striking—she is completely silent. And lastly, she always wears a skirt and a top. The perp tonight was wearing a hoodie pulled up over his head with tennis shoes and blue jeans with white spots on them."

Brock was silent for several minutes as he slipped into Prosecuting Attorney mode, the building blocks starting to stack into a coherent order in his brain. "Alright," Brock began, summing up the information, "so Carley's attacker and Jessica's murderer was trying to pawn this murder off as The Pusher's. He's definitely not law enforcement—if he didn't know about the gender issue. So then, why Cindy Grant? If he isn't going to acknowledge this murder like he did Jessica's, what is it about Ms. Grant that's so different and irrelevant to his motives, yet so necessary to permanently silence her and remove her from the picture? What is the connection?"

Chase added to Brock's observations, "The only implication we can come up with that makes sense is that maybe she saw or heard something she shouldn't have."

"Considering where her windows face, my guess is that she probably saw something she shouldn't have," Robyn chimed in. "It's possible she saw who left the panties and note on your roof garden. From what I've scanned so far of the letters, Ms. Grant references you in your garden a lot."

"That makes sense," Brock agreed, and Chase nodded. "How current are the letters you've found so far?"

"The most current one we've discovered so far is from about a week ago, September 29th," Robyn responded. "It references your more-than-deferential treatment of Carley as you bring her into your home—in less than complimentary terms."

Chase chuckled. "You know it. You really pissed her off that day, Brock. Maybe that's why the letters stopped so abruptly around that time."

"That makes sense," Robyn agreed, "but we'll keep looking. Everywhere we turn, there's more letters to find."

Brock smiled unhappily at Chase. "I've been so busy with Carley that I didn't even realize they had stopped coming. Did you call Joan to see if I had gotten any more at work?"

Robyn grimaced. "Well, I tried—but your personal assistant was a little miffed that you hadn't called her yourself. So, I'm not exactly sure. She pretty much hung up on me. I'm a little surprised she didn't call you herself."

"She may have," Brock acknowledged as he reached for his phone. "I haven't even scanned all my missed calls yet, let alone my messages."

As Brock dialed his voicemail, Robyn and Chase moved off to continue their search of Ms. Grant's apartment.

After deleting the nine calls from Chase, he came upon his personal assistant's strident yet competent tone.

"Brock, I'm not sure why I'm hearing this from Detective Hayes and not from you, but I will not be confirming or denying any personal correspondence you may or may not have received here at your office without your express permission. I assume you will call me at your earliest convenience. I hope you pass along my well wishes to Ms. Lyons."

Brock chuckled. Yep, Joan was a mama bear on steroids when it came to her domain—and by extension, his domain—and she in no way compromised her rules to kiss anyone's butt.

Brock dialed his office number while he shouted out to Robyn and Chase, "Yep, she called—and I'm calling her back now... Good afternoon, Joan. How are you?"

"That's wonderful," Brock responded to Joan's reply. "Yes, I did get your message—and I'm at the crime scene right now with Detective Hayes and Detective Braddock. They've identified the love letter writer, and it's linked in some way to the attack on Carley."

"Yes, Ms. Lyons—but you might as well get used to calling her Carley, as we are getting married shortly."

Chase and Robyn both appeared in their respective doorways with identical smirks on their faces. It occurred to Brock in that moment how much Robyn was coming to mean to him and Carley as a friend. A good friend.

Brock brought himself back into the present with a firm response to his assistant. "No, I don't believe it's too fast. In fact, it's been two years too long. Not that it should bother you in any way. More importantly, right now we need to know whether I've received any more of those anonymous love letters," he added shortly.

Brock turned his back on Chase and Robyn's laughter, which abruptly ceased with Brock's suddenly tense posture.

"There was? Have you opened it yet? Well then, read it to me!... Yes, Joan, I know, and I'm sorry. Would you please read it to me?... Thank you."

The alarm on Brock's face was apparent to the two detectives as they moved in on his position, eager to hear what the letter said.

"It's dated October 3rd,

'My Dearest Brock, How I long for the care, love, and devotion I see in your eyes when you look at her. Why does everyone love her so much? What does she have that I do not? I know that if you had just taken a little of your time to get to know me, you would be looking at me with all that care, love, and devotion. I know it in my soul.

One day soon, I'll work up the courage to walk up to you and give you that opportunity to love me. Soon—maybe sooner than I ever hoped. If that man who keeps climbing up to your garden is any indication, your would-be girlfriend may well have a new suitor she prefers—he is pretty buff. I've always admired his physique when he works out at The Gym.

So maybe, just maybe, I don't have the competition for your affections that I thought I had.

Always know you have me when she and Mr. Buff leave you high and dry.

Always yours, with all my love,

-Lady Love.'"

Before anyone could say anything, Joan continued:

"There's a postscript here as well. It says:

I had no idea he could ever be competition for you. Leaving panties and strange flowers on your roof garden seems like a really rude thing to do to me, but know that he'll never have my heart the way he seems to have Carley's. Be careful with your heart, Brock. xoxo

. . .

"Holy crap!" Chase exclaimed after a pregnant pause.

"She knows who it was that left the panties and those intricate paper flowers—but misinterpreted his act of leaving them. He also must have seen her watching from her window," Robyn mused, making copious notes in her notebook.

Brock took Joan off the speakerphone as he turned to speak to her while Robyn and Chase conferred. "Joan, I'm sending over a patrolman to pick up that letter. And—well, thanks for looking after me. But if another letter happens to come, please let Detective Hayes or Braddock know right away. Then call me, okay?... Thank you, Joan. I will pass along your congratulations to Carley... Take care. I'll see you soon."

Brock ended the call and turned back to Robyn and Chase. In unison, they all whispered:

"The Gym."

Chapter 7

Marrying Brock? Who does she think she is, marrying someone else when she has promised to love, honor, and cherish me forever? There must be some mistake—Ken the wonder idiot must have it wrong.

The way he's strutting around like a big peacock, spreading the lies to all who will listen that Carley is getting married to Brock in two days. There is no way my Carley would do that. Amnesia or not.

Instinctively, she must know she is mine. This has got to be some hair-brained scheme the police and Brock cooked up to keep them apart. Well, that won't happen.

But how? There's only one way he can think of now that the fire escape route has been denied him by the shiny new grate and lock. Sneaking in under their radar is risky and dangerous, but with the life—and wife—he planned for himself on the line, he doesn't really have a choice.

As he gets ready for his excursion into the enemy's camp—something he is well-trained for courtesy of the military—his anger builds to the point of accelerating his blood pressure. He needs to work off some of this stress before he explodes.

As he heads out of his house for a brisk walk to The Gym, he passes by the corner where he took care of Cindy Grant. He notices the crime scene tape and smirks to himself. Proud of how he handled the situation, no one would ever link Cindy to Jessica or Carley.

With his smug smirk firmly in place, he strides into The Gym just in time to see Bryan walk out of his office. For just a moment, he thought he saw inopportune questions in Bryan's eyes, but it couldn't be—it must be a trick of the lighting. His plans have all been perfect. A second glance in Bryan's direction shows him arguing on the phone with his latest conquest. Nothing to do with him after all. He walks over to the free weights and begins doing bicep curls, then maybe a jog on the treadmill, and then back home to eat dinner and head off to engage his plan to get Carley out of the evil clutches of Brock.

After all, tomorrow is going to be a momentous day. A day to be ready for. After all, tomorrow he will get his wife back—and be rid of Brockton Thorne the Third forever.

"So," Carley's lazy voice queried from the shelter of Brock's strong arms, "the fake wedding is tomorrow, right? Who knows it's fake? What about your parents? How are we going to get everything ready? When...?"

Brock pulled her even closer and landed a big smooch on her lips. He laughed and replied, "It's going to be fine, Sweetheart. Mom and Dad know it's fake, but they are on their way home anyway." Brock paused for another kiss, this one more thorough, "Dani and Chase know, as well as Detective Hayes—Robyn, I mean."

A third person—hidden below in Carley's office—pauses in stunned silence. From his position directly beneath Brock's closet, he hears it: Carley's unmistakable moan of passion, answered by Brock's own.

The only other sound is the soft, rhythmic whir of his small, old-fashioned hand crank drill, steadily boring holes through the ceiling directly below. . .

Oh, she is not kissing that conceited man... he mutters. *That stupid brat is cheating on me—thinking I'd never find out.*

His breath quickens with rage. *Well, fine. I know exactly how to punish her for this.*

***

Later that day, Carley, Brock, and Dani enter the Westcott Building lobby with big smiles and exhausted feet.

"Wow, I never thought you could get ready for a wedding in just one day. Well, not even that—it's only been half a day really." Carley was musing aloud again as she continued, "I wonder if the event coordinator has finished getting the roof garden ready yet? They promised to have everything ready by two p.m., right?"

Dani leaned over to whisper in Carley's ear, "Don't worry, everything will be ready—and it is going to be the loveliest fake wedding ever."

"Shhh, Dani...." Carley giggled and glanced around as she chastised Dani with a smile. "It will be real tomorrow night. Tonight is just for Mr. Psycho, as you well know—and it's supposed to be a secret!"

Bryan Hogan, the manager of The Gym, stepped out and asked Brock, "Have you seen Detective Hayes?"

Brock paused, looked at his girls, then back to Bryan. Seeing the look on his face, he returned his gaze to Carley and Dani. "Why don't you ladies head up to the penthouse. Security hasn't had any problems today—I checked just before we walked in. You can start getting yourselves ready, and, yes, I'll send Becca up as soon as she gets here. Just be sure to check the security camera before opening the door to anyone. Okay?"

Carley hesitated, but Dani tugged on her arm with gentle insistence. "Come on, Carley. You'll see him soon enough. Good grief, he's not flying to the moon, and we need every second we can squeeze out of the next few hours to get ready for your wedding—including a nap."

Carley's bright and shiny smile lit on Brock and then on Dani as she nodded her agreement.

"Good grief, girlfriend—not a kissy-face nap," Dani laughed with Bryan, "a *real* nap, chick." Dani's smile took any sting out of her words. "Don't forget you get a honeymoon tomorrow night, so try to be patient."

Dani pulled Carley to the stairs as Carley tried to get one more taste of Brock's lips, while Bryan held him in place, noting the adoring, goofy grin on his friend's face as he strained for that last taste as if it were his last.

A stab of jealousy wafted through him in a slow wave as he briefly wondered if that brand of love was ever going to find him—and how he would recognize it if he ever bumped into it.

When Carley was finally out of sight, Brock turned his full attention back to Bryan. "What's going on? Why are you looking for Robyn—I mean, Detective Hayes?"

"Well," Bryan began, "I'm not sure it means anything, but no one has seen Thomas today. Well, actually, no one has seen him since about eleven a.m. yesterday. He isn't answering his phone—in fact, it's off because every call is going straight to voicemail."

Brock's once-clear eyes turned to hurricane-force anger as he focused all his considerable energy directly upon Bryan. "Tell me everything."

***

Carley and Dani let themselves into the penthouse, and Carley made her way to the bedroom to deposit their bags on the bed when she first heard the squirrels chattering away. She frowned. Brock had Moose and Squirrel brought up the other morning and moved them into his living room. That alone should have kept them hiding in their pouch for days until they got used to their new surroundings.

Dani entered the room, breaking Carley's pensive thoughts. "I reset the alarm and grabbed you a soda."

"Thanks," Carley said absently as she realized the squirrels' chatter had a frantic quality to it—and as she listened more closely, she realized that they were scurrying all over their cage, in the middle of the day. *Something was wrong.*

Dawning horror was rising in Carley's eyes as Dani began to question her. "What...?"

Carley put a finger to her lips and grabbed Dani's hand, dragging her into Brock's office, pointing to the panic room door. Dani, catching on, understood immediately and bent to the task of opening the door just as they both heard a heavy tread hit the parquet flooring in the hall.

With a scared look at one another, the door to the panic room opened swiftly and silently as Dani grabbed Carley's hand. They strode quickly through the door and pressed the button to close it. Carley took the three steps through the walkway straight to the control console and hit the penthouse monitor button. As Dani came up beside her, they both stared at the screen in horror.

Carley was numb. She felt Dani grab her, but the full weight of her memories of that night came crashing down upon her much like a tightrope snapping suddenly under its walker's weight and sending her free-falling into the bottom of a great chasm. She slipped into unconsciousness just as the bottom of that great chasm came into horrible clarity.

Dani struggled with Carley's dead weight as she blacked out. With great effort, Dani finally got her over to the small bed at the far end of the room as the angry words came floating to her through the speakers at the control console.

"I know you're here, *wife*. You will *never* leave me again. Be a good girl and come to me now and I won't inflict as severe a punishment as last time. *Carley! Come. Out. Right. Now.*"

Dani reached to turn down the speakers as Thomas Mitchell, the friendly laundry manager, began to rip the penthouse apart, searching for Carley and hurling curses and promises of punishment.

Struggling to understand, Dani picked up the phone and dialed. *"Brock..."* she said, her voice barely steady.

***

Just as Bryan was about to launch into his explanation, Robyn walked into the lobby with a warrant in hand and a SWAT team striding in behind her.

She stopped short, recognizing Brock and Bryan, then headed over their way, ignoring their blatantly questioning and incredulous looks.

Over her shoulder she threw orders, "Captain Raydor, check The Laundry and The Gym. Let me know if he's there." Turning back to Brock and Bryan, she handed Brock the warrant and eyed them warily. "You've figured it out then, have you?"

Bryan responded before Brock could. "Thomas, right?"

Robyn gave Bryan a not-so-purely-assessing look. "Yep. We finally got a DNA hit from the military database that links him to Carley's bra and panties and the epithelial cells from around Cindy Grant's throat. That linked him to both murders and Carley's assault. Judge Warren issued the warrant for his arrest, and he issued multiple search warrants for his home, work, Carley's condo, and all the common areas of the Westcott Building. Sorry, Brock, I would have called and given you a heads-up, but everything has happened so fast, I haven't had a second to think."

"Don't apologize for doing your job. I'm thrilled by the progress you've made; feel free to search wherever you need to. Bryan?"

"Oh, yeah, feel free," Bryan roused himself from his very impolite stare at Robyn. "I don't think I locked our condo when I came down here, so please don't kick down the door."

Brock looked at Bryan sharply, then at Robyn and smiled but kept his own counsel. "I know that Mrs. Bruns is at her weekly poker game. Not sure about Jon, but just knock. I'm sure neither of them care if you search for a murderer in their condo. I doubt they would want to keep him."

"Now that you know the *who,* can you give us a rundown of the *what, when, where,* and *why?*" Brock's cautious elation was evident, but he wanted answers—more than he was getting.

Captain Raydor—*Ray* to his friends—the SWAT team leader, walked up to Robyn just then. Holding up a finger to signal that Brock and Bryan should give her a moment, she turned to Ray.

"Captain, what's the situation?"

"Detective Hayes, Mitchell isn't in The Laundry or The Gym. The Laundry is completely empty, and there are only three very startled patrons in The Gym, who are now leaving. What's next?"

Hayes nodded. "Post someone at all the exits, then start in the basement and work your way up. Mr. Bruns—the manager's son—will probably be cooperative, per Mr. Thorne and Bryan here. Bryan just informed me his condo is already unlocked, so be nice and don't break his door. He and Chase live across the hall from Ms. Lyons. Then, search the penthouse."

"Yes, Ma'am," Captain Raydor responded, "but considering the level of this guy's obsession with Ms. Lyons,

maybe we should call in some backup to search the surrounding area. I doubt he's very far. It's just a hunch, but
I think he's very close."

Robyn thoughtfully cocked her head as she pulled out
her phone to request backup, while Raydor gave his team
their assignments.

"Cutter, Mace, and Hicks—hit the alley and the two
exits there as well as the emergency exit at the back. Don't
forget the fire escapes and the sliding glass door behind
the hedge of the manager's condo. Bakker, take the front
entrance. Watch each other's backs—GO!"

Cutter, Mace, and Hicks hit the doors at a double pace
to take up their positions in the alley and rear of the building. Bakker took his station outside the front door.

Raydor continued handing out assignments as Robyn
wrapped up her phone call to the precinct and turned back
to Brock and Bryan. She inquired of Bryan, "How did you
come to the conclusion it was Mitchell?"

"Well, to be honest, it was mostly gut instinct that
something was seriously going wrong with him lately. He
was in The Gym a couple of days ago and as he ran on
the treadmill next to mine, he was muttering to himself a
bit. Nothing I could understand, mind you, but when I
realized he didn't have headphones in just jamming to his

tunes like usual, it crossed my mind that maybe his cheese was beginning to slide off his cracker a bit."

"That's it?" Robyn asked incredulously.

"No," Bryan said a bit defensively. "I noticed that he disappeared about eleven a.m. yesterday morning, right after you came to talk to Ken and looked through his daily logs again. As soon as you left, Thomas cornered Ken and grilled him about your conversation. Ken told him something about white flecks on the carpeting and in the foyer and black scuff marks." Bryan angled a cocked eyebrow at Robyn, who nodded her understanding and assent.

"Ken also passed on the good news of Brock and Carley's wedding this evening. When Thomas left without his usual snide remarks for Ken, he was pensive and distracted. The next time I came out to the lobby, about one p.m. or so, I noticed that The Laundry was closed and, well, you know—no one has seen Thomas since. At least no one that I've asked."

Bryan looked between a pensive Brock and a captivated Robyn, then asked Robyn, "What was it about those white bits of paper that struck you?"

Shaking herself out of her reverie, "Not paper, but soap flakes," Robyn responded as Captain Raydor's radio squawked.

"Detective," He interrupted quietly but succinctly, "you need to get up to Ms. Lyons' condo. You're gonna want to see this."

Robyn responded immediately. "We'll be right there." Knowing there wasn't a chance in the world she could keep Brock away, she added, "Come on, Bryan, you too. Your instincts and knowledge of Mitchell may help answer some questions for me."

As soon as they hit the stairs, Brock's phone rang. He stopped and looked at who was calling, and fear lit a raging firestorm in his eyes. "It's the panic room number," he told Robyn and Bryan as he answered the call, "What's happening?"

"Brock, it's Dani. Both Carley and I are in the panic room. Brock, it was Thomas—*Thomas.* How could one of our friends have done this?"

"I don't know, Squirt," Brock responded with what he hoped was a reassuring voice. "Are you okay? Is Carley?"

"Yes, we are physically okay. Thomas knows we entered the penthouse. We weren't exactly quiet about it, but he doesn't have any idea where we are. *He can't,* can he? You've never told him about the panic room, have you?" Dani was hysterical.

"No, honey. You, me, Chase, Carley, and Becca are the only ones who know it exists and how it works—well, except for now, Bryan and Robyn know of its existence also. Dani, how is Carley? Let me talk to her!"

"Oh Brock, I can't," Dani pleaded. "She passed out as soon as she saw it was Thomas on the monitor. I think she remembered the assault. I put her on the bed, but she is still unconscious, and I'm not waking her—that would be too cruel right now. Her mind obviously needs the oblivion unconsciousness provides."

Brock, Bryan, and Robyn continued up the stairs to Carley's condo while Brock stayed in the hall to keep Dani on the phone.

"Okay, Dani," Brock responded resignedly, "tell me what I need to know. How did he breach security?"

"I don't know, Brock. The door was locked and the security code was engaged. The security report left on the table by the door indicated every event planner and caterer that came in went out again. I assume that meant everyone was accounted for and verified by driver's licenses as well as their supervisor, whom you had already approved and provided an ID for."

"I also don't see anything remotely like an entry point for him on any of the monitors, so unless he snuck down from the roof somehow, I have no idea how he got in here."

"Well, crap... hold on, Dani," Brock interrupted her. "Robyn needs something. What's going on, Robyn?"

"We found out how he got into your penthouse and where he's been hiding since yesterday morning. Come on in and look, but be very quiet," Robyn warned.

Brock nodded to Robyn, then spoke into the phone. "Honey, I'm at Carley's condo. They figured out how Thomas got into the penthouse, but I need to go quiet for a bit. I won't hang up—I just need to listen for a few minutes, okay?"

"Brock, we're fine. We're safe here in the panic room, so stop worrying so much about us," Dani told him in exasperation. "I'm not the baby here, Baby Boy. I'm going to call Chase—I need him. Just call me back when you're done and let me know what's going on and what to do next."

"Dani..." Brock began, but he was speaking into dead air. He shook his head, pocketed his phone, and followed Robyn into Carley's condo, straight to the farthest bedroom that she had turned into a home office.

He stopped dead at what his eyes were trying to tell him. With only the light from the window, it took him a few moments to process what he was seeing.

Plaster dust coated every surface, and as his gaze traveled upward, he experienced a surge of anger so great he took several steps toward the hole in the ceiling before Bryan grabbed his arm and clamped his other hand over Brock's mouth, dragging him back through Carley's condo and into the hall.

"Son of a...!" Brock snarled. "Exactly where does that hole lead?"

Robyn answered him from behind. "Your closet, directly under the hanging rod at the back, next to a dresser. Essentially in the furthest corner."

"Oh crap!" Brock reiterated in a more moderate voice. "How did neither Carley nor I see a hole that big in the closet this morning?"

"Probably because it wasn't there yet," Robyn answered. "He used a small manual hand drill; it must have literally taken him hours. I'm sure he didn't break through until sometime late this morning. There is also evidence that he slept—or at least rested—for a while in Carley's bed and made himself comfortable in her kitchen as well. Judging by what we can hear him ranting up there, he, umm... well, he had enough holes drilled by last night to listen to every conversation."

Robyn hesitated, and Bryan came to her rescue. "He must have heard every conversation about your wedding."

"Oh crap." Brock realized how much more danger that put Carley in. "Yeah, we talked about it a few times last night. I'm sure that has put him over the top on the pissed-off scale. Thank God Carley and Dani are safe in the panic room. So, what happens now?"

***

Carley awoke slowly, eerily reminiscent of when she was coming out of her coma. Confused at first, she just lay where she was and listened to Dani talk, hoping for a clue to what was going on now, "Chase, I'm fine. Carley realized something was wrong in the penthouse almost immediately. It was spooky, actually, and we got to the panic room long before we ever saw him on the monitors. That was when Carley fainted."

Dani paused, presumably listening to Chase. "Yeah, I realize he must have heard us—we weren't exactly quiet when we got here."

During this second pause, all the memories came flooding back in. Carley audibly gasped and started panting, well on her way to a full-blown, PTSD-driven panic attack.

Dani noticed immediately and informed Chase, "I've got to go. Carley's awake and having a panic attack—call Brock for more info and let him know what's going on." Dani blurted out as she unceremoniously hung up on Chase and ran over to Carley to soothe her through her panic attack.

Thanking God that she had the foresight to put in a supply of Carley's medications yesterday during their tour, she grabbed an anti-anxiety pill, shoved it in Carley's mouth, and encouraged her to chew it while she popped the top of a can of Pepsi to help her wash it down.

Meanwhile, Carley, who was aware of her untimely panic attack, was cooperating as best she could through her panic and despair to get herself under control so Dani wouldn't be burdened with her blubbering self.

However, it was the sound of Thomas's scream of unfiltered rage over the open intercom that got Carley's attention the fastest and succeeded in stopping her panic attack before it could fully engage her mind and body.

Carley smiled at Dani as she got her breathing evened out, the tunnel vision receded, and that disturbing blind panic left her eyes. After a few moments, she sat up and asked Dani, "What's he doing out there? Does he know we are here—or where we are?"

Dani was looking at Carley carefully and, as she glanced over at the monitor briefly, she answered, "No, he didn't see us come in here, so basically, he's just trashing the penthouse and screaming at you and Brock for ruining his life and marriage. Apparently, you're a *whore* who gave away your *marriage* to him, and Brock's a *wife-stealing jackass* with *too much money* and *not enough sense to come in out of a storm*, etc., etc."

Carley emitted a genuine laugh. "Well, fiction can be fun... or not," she quoted as she stood and took in Thomas's appearance as he filled the screen. His features were grotesquely morphed by the nearness of the camera lens. "I think he found one of the cameras."

Carley's long-suffering sigh filled the room. "What do we do now?" she almost begged Dani for a coherent answer.

"I'm not sure," Dani replied, eyeing her warily, "but if they don't do something soon, he's going to completely destroy the penthouse." Dani paused to watch Thomas lick the camera, and both she and Carley shuddered as Thomas licked it again and winked grotesquely into the camera.

"I did call Brock first thing. He, Robyn, and probably more cops are downstairs at your condo doing something—and they know what's going on. I'm quite sure Chase is on his way also."

On instinct, Carley pressed the intercom button, yet paused, not quite sure what to say.

Thomas helped her out by licking the camera again and spewing out more bile about *wives who don't obey their husbands*.

Carley let her righteous anger mount at the sewage spewing out of the evil polluting his very soul. "You know," she began, "we have never gotten married, Thomas. We've never even dated. *Never will*. So, I'm a little confused as to why you think that we *are* married and have any such claims on my life?"

Thomas paused mid-rant and stopped licking the camera. A crafty grin spread across his distorted face, reminding Carley of why she *hated* clowns.

"I *knew* I heard you come in. Show yourself, *wife*... Carley, and no one else has to get hurt."

Thomas's tone was too calm, and Carley knew an eruption was coming—but all that mattered right now was keeping him occupied long enough for help to arrive, hopefully with a plan that she did not have beyond keeping him talking.

Carley snorted in derision into the intercom and calmly asked a question she knew would wind him up like a monkey on meth. "Okay, then, what was with those girly paper flowers? Did you make those yourself? Or did you have to buy them off the internet?"

Knowing a thunderstorm was coming, Carley quickly released the intercom button. That action alone flew Thomas—straight as a GPS-guided missile—back into his rage, gnawing at the camera's housing, trying to dig it out with his teeth apparently, or maybe dig his way *in here* with her, Carley thought warily.

Carley turned back to an awe-struck Dani and chuckled nervously. "Hey, remind me to hose that thing down with Lysol whenever we get out of here. *Ick.*"

"I'll keep him busy gnawing at the camera and all riled up. You call Brock and Robyn back and let them know what's going on up here. Hopefully they have a better plan than mine."

Startled, Dani giggled and replied, "Yeah, I kinda hung up on him to call Chase, so I need to update him and let him know that you are *more than okay*. You're *heroic* in a *comic book* sort of way."

Dani's gaze was caught by the monitor again. "What *is* with him licking and gnawing at the camera?"

"Anyway," Dani purposefully turned her back on the monitor to address Carley face to face, "I do know that Brock and the police think Thomas accessed the penthouse via your condo in some way, and they have to be quiet about investigating it—or I guess they think Thomas will hear them before they are ready."

Carley took a deep breath and replied, "Okay, I can work with that. Call Brock back and tell him that I'm okay and I will keep Thomas riled up and busy so they can do what they must do to capture him."

Dani looked doubtful. "I'm not so sure you should antagonize him further, Carley. He may get out of his ranting and licking zone right back into destroying-the-penthouse zone."

"That's what I'm counting on," Carley rejoined. "The louder he is, the easier it is for the police to get into the penthouse without being detected."

"Oh, well, yeah—*good plan* then." Dani turned around and picked up the phone and dialed Brock as Carley pressed the intercom button to engage the enraged Thomas once again.

***

The SWAT team began pulling themselves through the hole in the ceiling. The first officer up silently slid the pocket door of the closet closed to further mask any noise they made making the climb up.

Martinez, after closing the pocket door, reached down for Stewart, then Warren, until Captain Raydor pulled up Detective Hayes.

Eight well-armored and armed tactical officers crammed into Brock's closet and bathroom—enough to make even the stalwart Robyn a bit claustrophobic.

Everyone knew their job, so there was no need to con-
fer. Martinez silently slid open the pocket door and the
team began to move into the bedroom, preparing to take
Mitchell down.

Robyn and the team stopped to listen for clues to get
a fix on where Thomas was in the penthouse. As they
listened to Carley egg Thomas on—his angry, rutting bull
noises interspersed with the crash of dishes—Robyn whispered, *"Smart woman."*

Brock watched and listened from the top of Carley's
desk, just barely looking over the rim of the hole in his
closet—listening to Carley goad Thomas on and Thomas
smashing what sounded like every dish in the place. Right
at that moment, Brock's cell phone rang. For the space of
five seconds, no one moved or said a thing—dead silence
reigned in the penthouse as Brock hit the silence button
on his phone.

"It's too late!—GO!" Captain Raydor yelled at his team
as they heard Thomas's heavy tread run past them in the
hall.

Martinez reached the hall first, sweeping his rifle left to
right and spotting Mitchell bounding up the spiral staircase to the roof. *"Halt!"* he commanded, giving chase.

A second later, they heard the door to the roof slam
open as Thomas made his break to escape.

With eight SWAT team members and Robyn in pursuit, Thomas had little choice but to jump from the roof to the two-story building next door. His military training kicked its way through the haze of rage currently in charge of his brain as he tucked and rolled to freedom. He wasted no time looking behind him as he ran and jumped from one rooftop to the next, two of the most agile SWAT team members hot on his trail across the Lewiston skyline.

Meanwhile, Captain Raydor radioed his units on the ground to engage in the foot pursuit based on locations supplied by Martinez and Coolidge, who were tracking the progress from Brock's roof with scopes.

With two of his men pursuing Mitchell across the rooftops and another two tracking from above, Captain Raydor ordered his four remaining members back down to the truck to engage in this unusual perp pursuit—on wheels.

***

Dani, just realizing she had jeopardized Thomas's capture, hung up the phone—albeit too late. Both she and Carley watched helplessly as Thomas bounded up the stairs and out of their sight.

As they watched the SWAT team pursue Thomas up the stairs, Carley sighed. "That could have gone better. Brock always has his ringer on silent."

"Carley, I'm so sorry. I should have called Chase instead," Dani sighed.

"No," Carley soothed, "I told you to call Brock because we knew he was here already. Anyway, they're probably apprehending him on the roof. It's not like there are too many places to hide up there."

Dani and Carley watched the monitor as Robyn walked back into the bedroom closet and returned moments later with Brock. They made their way into the hall just in time to watch the five remaining SWAT team members run down the stairs and out the penthouse door.

"Well, that doesn't say good things, now does it?" Carley remarked sadly.

"No, it sure doesn't," Dani agreed, her voice laced with guilt.

Carley looked between the monitors, confused. "Where did Brock go?"

"Right here, Sweetheart," Brock answered as he sidled up behind her to embrace her. Carley jumped, then instantly relaxed into his powerful chest and sighed out her relief.

Not content with a hug from the back, she turned and hugged him fiercely. Brock, not to be outdone in their affectionate exchange, tipped her head back with his thumb under her chin and kissed her so soundly and thoroughly they missed the knocking on the front door—and Dani leaving the panic room to let Chase in.

Dani didn't hesitate but rushed into Chase's embrace and instantly broke down. Chase picked up the woman he loved more than his life and walked through the rubble into the living room, settling onto the couch with her on his lap as she cried out her frustration and recovered from the abrupt drop in adrenaline. As she sobbed, her heart tumbled out faster than her tears.

"I love you, Chase. I love you so much." Dani sobbed into his dress shirt, soaking it—and his chest—with her tears. She decided that no matter the past, Chase was her future. Chase stiffened, then pulled Dani tighter into his embrace and finally found that elusive moment of peace he'd been searching for since that fateful day in college.

While Brock was reuniting with Carley in the panic room and Dani was settling her future with Chase in the living room, Robyn stood in the middle of the foyer desperately trying to figure out the alarm system—just as it started blaring more mayhem.

Bryan, who cautiously crept up the stairs with Becca in tow, rescued her. Robyn ignored the tiny stab of jealousy she experienced noticing how Bryan held Becca's hand as he punched in the code to shut down the alarm system. Becca stared around in wonder before asking, "The wedding is off, I suppose?"

Robyn grinned a bit lopsidedly, which caused Bryan's heart to stutter, and replied, "Well, for today, anyway."

Bryan disengaged his hand from Becca's as he half asked, half stated, "So, Thomas got away. How did that happen?"

Robyn straightened her shoulders and cop mode was instantly back in place. "He jumped the roof. Two of Raydor's men pursued. He left two stationed on the roof with high-powered scopes and rifles. Though from what I hear, he's already out of sight. The foot pursuit is over, and they're calling in the chopper to begin an aerial search and set up blockades. Crap, this is going to be a huge media storm—let alone all the paperwork. I hate paperwork."

Just then, Robyn's phone rang. A new report came in. She stepped away to take it as Martinez and Coolidge came down the stairs from the roof garden to report. She clicked off her phone and faced the men.

"What's the status?"

"Captain assigned us here to provide you backup and protection detail until Mitchell is apprehended," Martinez informed her. "He's in the wind. We thought we caught up with him when he started backtracking in this direction, but it was some old dude walking his dog. Blockades are going up on all major and minor roads. The chopper is in the air with a spotlight, and a canine unit is on its way. He won't stay hidden for long. Captain even sent a patrol unit back to his house in case he bolts there. Although with what we now know about his training, that doesn't seem likely."

"What doesn't seem likely?" Brock asked as he and Carley entered the penthouse from the back entrance of the panic room.

"Cool!" Martinez and Coolidge breathed as the secret door behind the deceptively positioned statue opened and closed, emitting Brock and Carley.

Robyn jumped at Brock's voice, startled, as Bryan chuckled and grabbed Robyn's hand, rubbing it in sympathetic, soothing circles that evened out her breathing—for all of five seconds—before it began galloping along with her pulse. But she didn't remove her hand from his.

Everyone seemed frozen in place, not knowing what to do, when Chase's yell from the living room galvanized them into action.

"Why don't you all come in here for an update from everyone at the same time so we can all be on the same page. I'm not moving."

Brock turned to reactivate the alarm on the door. Carley went into the kitchen to gather drinks for everyone, dragging Becca along to help. Robyn, Coolidge, and Martinez each picked up pillows from the living room furniture and took them in with them, while Bryan went up to the roof access, closed it as best he could after Thomas had busted it open, and reset the alarm code so they'd at least have some warning if someone opened it.

As he came back down the stairs, he intercepted Brock.

"You need to call Ken ASAP and get him up here with his trusty tools and a new lock for the roof access door."

With only a grimace, Brock pulled his phone from his pocket and dialed.

"Ken, it's Brock. I need you to bring your kit and a new lock for my roof access door. It got kicked in during Thomas's pursuit by the police and it's in serious need of repair before we can stay here. Can you come right up? Thanks, Ken. Just knock—we're all in the living room and I'll hear you. Half an hour or so for the hardware store? No problem. We'll see you in about an hour or so then. Thanks again, Ken."

As Brock hung up, he walked into the living room, spotted his fiancée, and made his way over the debris to pull her up and sit back down with her in his lap, much like several days ago—only now, the paramedics were replaced by two burly SWAT team members.

Dani broke the ice by setting an array of beverages on the coffee table. "Everyone, please help yourself. If you don't see something you prefer, let me know and I'll see if Brock has it."

Most everyone made a grab for something on the tray, murmuring their thanks. But it was Robyn who broke the stilted silence,

"Okay, here's what we know. First, we have a DNA match to Carley's attacker." Robyn shot a small, inquisitive smile at Carley, who nodded for her to continue. "A match with both Jessica Turnbull and Cindy Grant's murders. I've connected the white flakes found on the stairs after Carley's attack to The Laundry—and Mitchell in particular. They were soap flakes, not paper as some assumed," as she nodded to Carley, "I've checked Ken Harm's logs thoroughly. He also concluded they were soap flakes and even gave Mitchell a warning about it in the past. Going back six months, I found three instances in Ken's logs.

I also had the lab analyze the scuff marks that original-
ly caught Ken's attention that day. They came back as a
specific brand and style of work boot tread that matches
the exact kind Mitchell wears. It was part of my warrant
to collect his boots for comparison—though we'll still run
the comparison for court, we don't need it anymore to
make our case. Mitchell has done that for us."

Robyn paused and looked around. "Are there any questions at this point?" She gathered her thoughts. "Everything seemed to fall into place in one giant piece between
last night at Cindy Grant's home and this afternoon here.
Give me just a minute to put things in order."

As Robyn ordered her thoughts, Bryan stood up from
his position in the far armchair and crossed the room to the
chair Robyn was sitting in. He settled onto the arm and
gently began rubbing her shoulders in an effort to relieve
some of the afternoon's tension while she gathered her
thoughts. Much to his satisfaction, he realized it wasn't
working—the pulse in her neck leapt at his touch.

Good, he thought. She's not as unaffected as she pre-
tends to be.

Taking it as a sign, he got up and moved around to the
back of the chair, continuing the massage from a safer distance—for her sanity. As Robyn closed her eyes and rolled
her neck and shoulders in quiet appreciation of Bryan's

gesture, he glanced up and found a room full of friends and acquaintances grinning back at him. They were all well aware of what was happening between them.

Much to his delight.

Abruptly, Robyn stood, putting physical distance between herself and Bryan as she struggled to regain composure. She paced slowly, reclaiming the mental clarity of her much-needed police detachment and logic—without embarrassing either herself or Bryan with more public displays of affection.

But just as she looked up to resume her recap, her eyes locked with Becca Love's.

Becca was watching her—watching them—with clear confusion and the unmistakable shimmer of hurt before she managed to mask it.

Caught, Becca gave Robyn a knowing smile.

An unexpected and unwanted shaft of jealousy bolted through Robyn's nervous system without remorse or dignity.

Well, Robyn mused to herself in a corner of her mind, if that's the way he plays... I'm glad I let it get no further than a bit of flirtation.

With that, she squared her shoulders and began her explanation of the crime's sequence of events for everyone.

Chapter 8

That ungrateful, hateful woman! Thomas was livid as he stalked around Cindy Grant's apartment, secure in the knowledge that it was the very last place anyone would ever look for him. *She was in that penthouse. I know she was there with that witch Dani. But where?*

Doesn't matter anymore, he fumed. *I'll never be able to get that close again.*

Thomas paced back and forth in Cindy's living room, muttering to himself. He knew what must happen now. He only had one option left. *If she cannot be mine, she won't belong to anyone. Especially Thorne.*

His pacing became more and more agitated. *Surely, they won't have a wedding tonight. But if I know how impatient*

Thorne is, it'll be very soon. Maybe even tomorrow. Which leaves me very little time to prepare.

As soon as things calmed down outside, he would go to one of his stashes and get what he needed to finish this final piece of business with Carley—so he could get on with his life. After all, I shouldn't have to be alone. And I have a new wife to find... and school in the ways of propriety.

Night fell, and Thomas sat alone in the murdered woman's apartment, plotting his new life. Plans where it would be, and what steps needed to be made to ensure his next wife never left him.

On the upside, being a widower always seemed to attract a horde of women looking for a husband of good quality, much like himself.

Life would be good again.

An evil, awful grin spread across his face as he sat there, staring into the fragile starkness of his imagination—someplace so dark, demons danced in delight.

The Next Day

After all the revelations last night with Robyn, Carley was more world-weary than she could ever remember being—even in the hospital. So much destruction of life over an obsession with her.

How was she ever supposed to get past something like that? For her, that was more horrifying than the attack she could now remember with dreadful clarity. Two beautiful young women had lost their lives over Thomas's obsession.

Brock was right. He had gently brought up therapy for her. At first reluctant, she was now certain he was right. She couldn't live her life haunted this way. It wasn't fair to Brock or their future children. It wasn't fair to her. *I'll find a good therapist after the honeymoon,* she decided.

With much to rejoice about, Carley decided to push the ugliness of the past couple of weeks away and concentrate on her wedding and honeymoon. There would be plenty of time for therapy when they got back from Hawaii.

A very impatient Becca interrupted Carley's musing. "Are you even listening to me, Carley? Because I would swear you weren't even in the room if I couldn't see you. Are you okay?"

Becca's brand of gruff and tender almost brought Carley to tears. "I'm sorry, Becks. I guess I was just glooming and dooming it for a bit and got a little lost in it. Sorry, Sweetie. I'm okay now. I've decided that I'm just going to shove it into a dark corner until after the honeymoon, and then seek out some biblical counseling."

Becca eyed her best friend through the dressing table mirror, then offered her a smile and a quick hug from behind. "It is okay to just let it go for a while and be happy with your life right now. However, if you start having nightmares or panic attacks, then it might be a good idea to pull it out of that dark corner and let some bright sunshine—via Brock—on it, burning away the darker edges. My guess is that you're suffering from PTSD, and you can't run from that for long, nor should you want to. Trust me on that one, Car's. Now enough of your doom and gloom—that's not what I asked you."

"Oh, right. Sorry. What did you ask?" Carley responded with a bit of a blush.

Becca swatted Carley's tush. "I asked if you like your hair this way. Not that we have any time to change it if you don't. And Brock's parents are in the hall and would like to come in to see you for a few minutes before the ceremony."

"Oh!" Carley exclaimed as she really looked at herself in the mirror. "Oh Becca, it's so intricate and exquisite. I absolutely love it. Thank you."

Carley's strawberry-red hair was delicately intertwined in the tiara Brock had gifted her with earlier that day, displaying her hair and neck eloquently—which in turn displayed the sapphire stones in her earrings and necklace. Brock had pulled them out of his safe, telling her that he had bought them for her about a year ago just because he thought they would look so lovely on her.

They encompassed her *something blue*. Her *something new* was, of course, the tiara. *Something old* was one of her mother's old lace handkerchiefs she had managed to save through all the turmoil of her youth. And finally, *something borrowed* belonged in a freak show.

Becca had insisted that Carley must have a splash of color in her wedding, so she loaned her one bright fuchsia heel that matched her custom colored walking boot. *Having it thrust upon her* was more accurate, but Carley was in a generous mood and let Becca's enthusiasm slide. Carley would get Becca back at her own wedding one day.

At the dressing room table where she sat, lost in her reflection of Becca's artistic arrangement of her hair and makeup, Carley failed to notice that Becca had let Brock's parents into the room.

Carley jumped in her seat when her reverie was interrupted.

"Oh darling, you look utterly gorgeous!" Louisa Mae exclaimed in her genteel Southern drawl. "You are going to steal the show, darling, and you deserve to."

Carley carefully tightened her robe around her body as she rose to meet her new in-laws. She was immediately pulled into the firm embrace of Brockton Senior, who declared with pride as he gazed down at Carley's smiling and slightly befuddled countenance, "Leave it to my boy to get to the prettiest girl in the city—present company excluded, my dear," he modified according to his wife's stern and loving glance.

As he let Carley slip from his exuberant embrace, he continued, pride evident in his voice, "And he arranged a wedding within three days. That boy sure knows how to go after what he wants—apart from the two-plus-year hiatus from his common sense where you were concerned, dear. I don't know what that boy was thinking, making you both wait that long when there was obviously love there all along. It does remind me of someone else I know. You too, Darling?" He kissed his wife's hand, and to Carley's utter fascination, she watched Louisa Mae blush under her husband's loving gaze.

"Now Brockton, you hold onto that flirting for later. Today is for our son and new daughter," Louisa Mae admonished with a private smile for her husband. "You're going to scare her off before Brock can get her to the pastor. And then you will pay handsomely, my dear."

Becca and Carley grinned at each other over Louisa Mae's head as she took over the room with the formidable grace only a Southern Belle could pull off.

"Now Brockton, you go on down to Chase's condo and see how Brock is getting on. I'm going to help Carley get into that heavenly dress so Rebecca can get ready also. Now scoot."

"Yes ma'am," Brockton Senior replied with a grin as he walked out the bedroom door, sliding it closed softly behind him.

"Now dear," she cooed at Carley, "let's get you into that sinfully gorgeous dress. We have fifty minutes and counting down." Louisa Mae admonished them in her dulcet yet firm drawl.

Becca, twittering a wave to Carley with her patented smirk firmly in place, turned into the dressing room/bathroom to get her own hair and makeup done and into her own gown.

"Now dear," Louisa Mae continued, "let's get you ready. We don't want to keep everyone waiting on us now, do we, hmm..."

Carley shrugged out of her silk robe and stood there a bit embarrassed in her new lacy and racy white lingerie—and that accursed fuchsia heeled shoe and her walking boot.

Louisa Mae turned with Carley's dress in hand and came to an abrupt stop at the sight of that footwear. She looked at Carley's mortified face and grinned. "I'm going to guess *something borrowed*, and if it's something else, I don't want to know about it."

Louisa Mae smiled and without another word, she gently lifted the gown from the bottom, coming up from the middle to lift it carefully over Carley's hair and makeup.

Having gotten the bodice over her hair and face, Louisa Mae pulled the two halves together in the back and hooked the top eye hook, then began weaving the lacing down the middle, leaving small peeks of Carley's back exposed from the top of the sleeveless dress down to her tailbone, ending in a small bow.

When Louisa Mae finished, she stood back to admire the fit and style of the princess waist gown.

Slowly, Carley turned toward the mirror as Becca came out of the dressing room needing help with her zipper—only to halt mid-stride and let out a small gasp at the glow literally coming from Carley.

"Oh. . . Wow! You're gorgeous!" Becca breathed out reverently as Louisa Mae smiled and replied, "Why yes, she very much *is* the glowing, radiant bride we all wish to be."

With a large and generous smile, Louisa Mae hugged Carley and whispered, "Well then, my love, what are we waiting for? Let's get you married so I can start planning for my future grandchildren."

It didn't seem possible, but Carley found herself blushing even harder as Louisa Mae hurried to Becca to help her zip her gown.

"We cannot go yet," Becca realized. "Dani hasn't come up yet from Chase's, and oh—she has all the flowers and is supposed to let us know when the guys are up in the garden ready for us."

"I'm here, with flowers in hand and news of the men and guests all accounted for and in place—except for you, Mother." Dani's smile lit the room. "Wow, you both look gorgeous and I'm not nearly ready yet—my hair's a mess. Hi, Mother, Daddy said you booted him out and injured his pride all in the same breath. I scooted out of there before I got trapped in a corner listening to his side of the tale. I let the guys take care of him."

"Take a breath, darlin'," Louisa Mae chuckled. "Let's see what we can do with your hair, dear."

***

The wedding was as beautiful as it could be because of its radiant bride and gallant groom. Handkerchiefs appeared as tears fell and smiles were abundantly given. Good cheer everywhere.

Everywhere except with those keeping watch for Thomas Mitchell to make his expected appearance.

Three SWAT team members were behind the ten-foot hedge with the patio furniture, keeping watch on the three sides they had access to, including the access ladder that had been unlocked for safety purposes.

Robyn and Captain Raydor were among the guests and undercover. Chase was in the wedding party—and undercover too.

By the time the groom thoroughly and shamelessly kissed his bride to oblivion, everyone watching for Thomas was getting edgy. They all knew he was coming, and now it would be sooner rather than later.

By the time the caterers had dinner ready in the dining room, all the police personnel—and Brock—were getting nervous, wondering when and where the attack would come.

But Carley's wedding day would proceed as smoothly as possible—or whomever disrupted it would answer to Brock.

When the guests and wedding party had taken their seats, Chase raised his glass of champagne for the best man's toast,

"While I have yet to take that long walk down the aisle, let it not be said by anyone who knows and loves Brock and Carley that the path can be as long as you make it or as short as you desire it. In Brock and Carley's case, both can be said. They each loved each other from afar for over two long years. Then *wham!* As soon as love is declared—within a short three weeks—here we are, celebrating with them their openly and uniquely declared love till the end of time.

May your paths always be made straight. May your hurts always be few, and may your love never dim or grow weary. To Faith. To Hope. To Love. I give you both over to an enduring friendship, courtship, and family love—Brockton Daniel Thorne the Third and Carley Leigh Thorne, everyone. *Cheers!*"

Cheers and many tapping of crystal flutes ensued as everyone there celebrated Brock and Carley's wedding day. All were swept up in the romance of Chase's toast.

All except Dani, who looked decidedly troubled.

When the party settled and the wait staff served dinner, Chase kept looking down the table at Dani, hoping to catch her eye, but noticed that she kept her head down and avoided his glances altogether.

When the cake was being served, Dani stood and excused herself, wanting a few moments to collect herself—but she should have known better. As soon as she turned into the hall, Chase caught up with her, "What's worrying you, love? I was hoping to ask you a very important question tonight."

The blood visibly drained from Dani's face and she began stuttering, "Wwh...aat? What do you?... What can you possibly mean, Chase?"

Chase frowned as he fingered the velvet jeweler's box in his jacket pocket, "Love, I think you *know* what question I mean. I wanted to wait till Mitchell was apprehended, but it's looking more and more like he's a no-show for tonight. I must say, that does surprise me a bit."

Dani began shaking her head in earnest, dislodging several of the pins holding her hair in place, "No, Chase. Please don't ask that of me. My answer will always be *no.*"

At Chase's shocked and bewildered face, Dani quickly hastened to add, "I can no longer deny the love I have for you, but that doesn't change my feeling on marrying you. I can never marry you, Chase. Please don't ask—please—you have my love. Openly and freely now, but marriage? *No.*"

Chase's shock and bewilderment slowly turned to anger and frustration, "*Why not?*" he hissed at her, mindful of the room full of friends and family just a doorway away.

"Chase..." Dani placed her hand on his arm, desperately trying to calm him and regretting getting into this discussion now. "You've always known this—why are you so surprised and angry *now*?"

Chase didn't even know how to answer such an absurd question. *Just yesterday* Dani was pledging her undying love for him. *Today* Brock was reminding him, not very subtly, what a stand-up guy he knows Chase to be. As if he hadn't been asking Dani to marry him for years now. *And now, it's still no?*

What the heck? was all he could think to say—still so stunned he was almost glad when his cell phone rang and took his focus off Dani and onto something else.

He glared at a defiant Dani as he yanked his phone from his belt and snapped, "Braddock!" to the poor soul on the other end of the line.

"I'll be right there," he growled as he snapped his phone onto his belt, hanging up on whomever had the misfortune to be on the other end of his line.

To Dani he only said, "We are in no way through with this conversation. If you disappear on me again, this time I *will* hunt you down to whatever slice of dirt you drag yourself and your camera off to. Do you understand me?"

Dani mutely nodded as Robyn came around the corner and stopped short at the near-murderous look in Chase's eyes and the clearly defiant one in Dani's.

"Well, *so* sorry to interrupt, but I just received a call and I need to respond to a scene."

Startled momentarily out of his anger toward Dani, Chase looked at Robyn. "Me too. It seems *The Pusher* has struck again on the corner of Second Street and Adams."

Robyn gaped at him. "That's where I've been called to respond also. Apparently, Mitchell has been spotted... Oh good Lord. It couldn't be *that* simple, could it?"

Understanding broke over Chase. "Well, if I know The Pusher at all, I'd say yes. Her profile suggests she would *not* like to have someone copycat her and try to place the blame for a victim's murder on her that she did *not* do. She believes she is on a mission from God, as suggested in her letters, and she's not shy about claiming her victims. In fact, she's *very* proud of her victims and the justice she and God mete out to the sinners—as she calls them. So yeah, I think what you're thinking is very possible—*even probable*. Let's go check it out."

As Chase turned away from Dani to leave, Robyn turned toward her and asked her to relay a message to Brock. "Would you please fill him in and tell him and Captain Raydor that we will call from the scene with confirmation of this victim being Mitchell or not? Raydor and his team will stay until the all-clear is given by his superior—but they know that. Thank you, Dani."

Robyn turned to follow Chase out the door.

"No problem," Dani replied, relieved to have even a brief reprieve from Chase's anger.

It flashed briefly through Dani's mind to take the coward's way out—call the magazine and take whatever overseas project they currently had handy. But no... Chase would just follow her. She was *quite* sure he meant what he said. That didn't mean she had to wait around here to face his wrath. She'd give Brock the message, extend her congratulations once again, then high-tail it home. Or maybe to a hotel until she felt up to facing Chase again.

Dani turned back to the dining room and spied Becca coming out of the guest bath with a smirk distorting her pretty face.

"You know," Becca began, "running away solves nothing—except maybe making him sweat a bit. However, if that's your goal and you just want a place to bolt for a while, I *do* have a guest bedroom, and I doubt he would ever think to look for you at my place."

Dani opened and closed her mouth. She didn't really know Becca, but they had been bonding through Carley these past couple of weeks, and she really *wanted* a couple of days to shore up her resolve.

"Thanks, Becca. If you really mean it, I'd love to get to know you better—and have a few Chase-free days to gather myself before confronting the coming storm."

"Of *course* I mean it," Becca replied. "And I would *love* to get to know you better also. I'm ready to go whenever you are. All that mushy love crap is getting so deep in there, my feet are getting wet. I *don't* do that nonsense, and Carley knows it. I do believe we fulfilled our wedding obligations; all pictures have been taken, and cake suitably stuffed into Brock's face. Besides, I'm sure they would *rather* be alone." Becca added with a waggle of her eyebrows to make Dani laugh.

"Oh, I do hope they got a picture of cake shoved up Brock's nose. I'd love to have seen that," Dani lamented.

"That's better." Becca laughed with Dani and, with another eyebrow waggle, added, "Your face is *very* expressive. Now you can face everyone without raising too many questions as to why you and Chase were out here for so long."

Becca and Dani entered the dining room smiling and giggling like two schoolgirls on laughing gas—much to everyone's amusement.

Dani casually walked over to Brock and whispered Robyn's message in his ear, then turned to the room in general. "Well folks, the deed is done and it's time for this Cinderella to head on home before the pumpkin hour. *Congratulations*, you two," she said as she leaned in, hugging Brock, then Carley. "Love you, Mother, Daddy—I'll see you all later."

Everyone seemed to take her departure as the hint they were all waiting for to make a mass exodus. All except Captain Raydor, who slid behind the Chinese screen into the living room as unobtrusively as possible while Brock and Carley said their goodbyes to their guests at the front door.

Raydor kept watch from the darkened living room, but his gut was telling him the danger was past. Never one to shirk his duty, he commed his team for sit-reps from each. After getting the all-clear he expected, he stood at attention and waited until the last guest left before coming out of the living room.

As he entered the hall, his phone rang, startling Carley into a yelp of surprise. Mouthing a *sorry* to her and Brock, he answered his phone. "Raydor here."

As he listened, Brock's own phone rang from the bedroom. As Brock walked into the bedroom to answer his phone, he glanced back at Raydor, who was finishing up his call.

"Thank you, Detective, for the sit-rep. I'll send the team home, and I'll meet you at the scene."

Brock and Carley's eyes widened at the implication in Captain Raydor's words, and Brock noted Chase's number on his caller ID. He listened to Chase's brief explanation, and a predatory gleam appeared in his eyes as a wide, satisfied smile spread across his mouth.

He replied to Chase, "Well, at least she saved the people of Lewiston the expense of a trial and incarceration. I

won't forget that when it comes time to prosecute her. Not
that I'll probably get the chance, with my now personal
connections to her." He hugged his wife. "It is so *worth* it
though, don't you think?"

From Brock's grin, Carley and Ray assumed Chase
agreed with him. Hanging up his phone, he exchanged a
nod with Raydor, then turned Carley into his arms tighter.

"It's over, Sweetheart. Mitchell is *dead.*"

As if it were the only thing holding her up, Carley sagged
with relief as the tension she had been carrying around all
day left her body all at once.

Raydor commed his men on the roof: *all clear.* Moments later they all trooped down the stairs and through
the hallway to the door, offering their double congratulations to the happy and now stalker-free couple on their
way out.

"It's over? He's dead?" Carley asked into the ensuing
silence.

"Yes, Sweetheart. It's really over. And he is really dead."
Brock set the alarm at the front door after the SWAT team
leader closed it behind himself, then climbed the stairs to
lock and key in the code there as well.

The four remaining wait staff and the two event plan-
ners/caterers—Marty and Karen—attending to their wedding and dinner, were furiously working to get everything

cleaned up so they could also get out of the newlyweds' way as soon as possible.

As Brock came back down the stairs, noting that all the food had been put away, he told the catering team that the rest of the dishes could wait until tomorrow—*late* tomorrow.

With the table clear and a load of dishes already running in the dishwasher, Marty made sure all the food was properly secured. They all loaded up with crates to take back to their kitchen and offered their congratulations. They made their way out the door Brock courteously held open for them.

As Marty passed him by, Brock handed over a very generous tip he knew would be split evenly. Marty was nothing if not fair to his employees.

As soon as the door closed behind them and the code reengaged, Brock swept up a still shell-shocked Carley and carried her off to their marriage bed...

...and the rest of their lives together.

The Pusher walks casually toward the crosswalk, having stalked her prey on his way to seek his own revenge. Little does he know that he has so little control.

Her thoughts are centered on God's own revenge.

She had been given all the control. The power over life and death for every person she encountered.

And dear Thomas... he was going to wish he had never crossed her path.

She walked up behind him, headphones in, her iPod playing The Devil Went Down to Georgia. A fitting song, she thought, for the little bit of revenge she'd been engaged to carry out.

The Pusher.

She chuckled to herself.

The creativity of the media was endless and imaginative—but also accurate. Hmmmm. She liked it. A lot.

A bus approached. She studied the driver—too alert, eyes scanning the street and every pedestrian.

No. He wouldn't work. He'd brake too soon to guarantee death. He might even be able to describe her to the police.

She could never understand these drivers who seemed determined to avoid her righteous work.

Didn't they see she was doing God's work?

Patience—her one remaining virtue—granted by God for this season of open punishments on sinners—had served her well. She could wait for the perfect vehicle.

One would come. It always did. It always would.

The light changed. She followed at a careful distance behind Thomas, doing nothing to spook him. Even with his ratty tennis shoes, torn jeans, that hoodie, and the too-full backpack, she knew exactly who he was—and likely what he carried inside that bag.

Naughty boy.

She'd been watching him for two days. When the police lost him last night, she was the one who figured out where he had fled. And she'd been on his trail ever since.

The idiot had dared to try and copy her.

And Heaven knew—nobody got away with that.

No one crossed God and walked away unscathed.

Her family, her so-called friends... they learned that lesson the hard way.

Well—except her brother. She'd always had a soft spot for the little guy. He wouldn't hurt anyone.

At the next intersection, it was just Thomas, her, and a businessman too distracted by his newspaper to notice anything. And mercy of mercies—her patience had paid off.

Four blocks from his intended destination, judgment arrived on a silver platter.

She smiled. God's humor was divine. She chuckled softly to herself as she braced her feet, positioning herself for the shove that was fated—therefore sinless.

If God didn't have a great sense of irony, Carley would have died at this very intersection when she pushed her all those months ago. But Carley had survived the vengeance—hers and God's.

So she was redeemed.

Apparently, God had found some future use for her after all.

  But Thomas wouldn't be so lucky.

  She reached out and gave him a hard shove—right into the path of the oncoming vehicle.

  She heard the satisfying thunk.

The crunch of his skull meeting pavement... and the final crack as the wheels of Justice—disguised as a city garbage truck—finished the job.

  She walked casually down the block, disappearing into the sea of people rushing to help. And she waited.

  Waited for the whisper in her ear.

Waited for God's next assignment.

His next bit of vengeance.

  The Pusher.

  God alone knew... she so loved the name He had chosen for her.

***

Carley and Brock's love story has come to a close... but a new one is just beginning. Stay tuned for Dani and Chase's.